The MASKED RIDER

Tales of the Wild West

AIRSHIP 27 PRODUCTIONS

The Masked Rider: Tales of the Wild West Volume Two

"Thunder at Devil's Tower" © 2014 Erwin K. Roberts
"Vultures of the Yellow Mesa" © 2014 Bill Craig
"The Hunting Party" © 2014 Roman Leary

An Airship 27 Production
Airship27.com
Airship27Hangar.com

Editor: Ron Fortier
Associate Editor: Gordon Dymowski
Marketing and Promotions Manager: Michael Vance

Cover illustration © 2014 Andy Fish
Interior illustrations © copyright 2014 Tom Rubalcava
Production and design by Rob Davis

ISBN-13: 978-0692239827 (Airship 27)
ISBN-10: 0692239820

Printed in the United States of America

10 9 8 7 6 5 4 3 2 1

THE MASKED RIDER
Tales of the Wild West
Volume Two

THE MASKED RIDER

"Thunder at Devil's Tower"

by Erwin K. Roberts

Three horses crested the hill some miles to the north of Wright, Wyoming. All three steeds carried saddles, but only two held men. The mighty coal black stallion's back served to carry a few bags and supplies.

Blue Hawk, the Yaqui, scanned the land spread out below him from the back of his Sorrel. Seeing no immediate problems, he let himself relax. At least as much as he ever did. He now looked for the pleasure of it. The Creator Of All Things, whether the Great Spirit, or he whom the whites called Dios, or God, surely worked long and hard to make so many different lands. These grasslands with dark mountains, so different from his home in what the whites called Mexico.

Blue Hawk's companion pulled binoculars from the saddlebags of his wiry looking Pinto. With them he scanned the horizon, obviously trying to find something. Then his face lit up.

"There it is," said the white man. He handed the instrument to his friend. "On the horizon, above the notch in the next hill."

Blue Hawk put the binoculars to his eyes. In the distance a dark shape stood well above its surroundings. The sides of it seemed almost sheer.

"What is that, Señor?"

"The Lakota call it 'Bear's Lodge Butte'; whites say it is 'The Devil's Tower.' Climbs more than twelve hundred feet above its base. Always wanted to see the thing up close."

"Perhaps when we finish in Pierre, Señor"

"Perhaps. But I want to..."

Almost directly in line with Devil's Tower a huge ball of smoke, dirt, and a spit of flame heaved itself into view. A moment later a crack of sound assaulted their ears. A hand seemed to slam against their chests.

The two men worked swiftly to calm their horses. The roiling ball continued to rise for hundreds of feet.

"Dynamite, Señor?" asked Blue Hawk.

"A lot of it, then, my friend. Let's go see what happened. Somebody may need help, or burying."

With that the two men urged the three horses ahead. Blue Hawk wondered, as he often did, which one of his friends would be needed. Wade Morgan, the wandering waddy, or the Hand of Justice called The Masked Rider.

Down the hill and up the next rise they hurried. They slipped through the notch and onward. At the crest of the third hill they paused to look things over.

"Look, Señor," pointed Blue Hawk. Not twenty yards to their left lay the tongue assembly of a heavy wagon. Bits of the wood smoldered.

"Tarnation! We best be glad everything's had time to fall outta the sky."

"I hope you are right, Señor."

"You and me, both. This way."

Soon almost every yard they traversed contained smoking bits of debris. Here a part of a wooden crate. There a crushed tinned bucket. Once a small keg of cigars that had been intact. Until it landed.

"Another wheel there," said Blue Hawk.

"That means we're dealing with several wagons, Hawk. And at least one of them held nothing but explosives. Can't be no other way. Less somebody's invented something way stronger than dynamite.

"Isn't that a road coming down that hill to the east? Then the blast must have come from over this little rise... Dear Lord!"

Before them now lay a narrow stretch of grassland. It ran about four hundred yards wide and nearly a mile long. A road of sorts roughly paralleled a dry gully until a simple wooden bridge crossed it. Several boulders blocked the bridge. Three hundred yards from the bridge the road had been replaced by a smoking crater over twenty feet wide and as deep as a proper grave. Of the wagons on either side of the crater only kindling remained. A couple of wheel hubs connected by a twisted axel marked the next place in the line toward the bridge. The wagon closest to the bridge lay on its top. Shattered wheel spokes pointed into the air as a small amount of smoke curled from underneath. Two wagons at the rear seemed to have been dismantled. Boards and cargo lay everywhere.

" Señor, where are the bodies? No horses. No men."

"Tarnation! You're right. Where are they?"

Blue Hawk scanned the scene again. Then a small motion caught his eye.

"In the gully," he pointed.

"Praise be! They had time to unhitch and run for cover. Some are still alive. We'll need the big medical kit and..."

Blue Hawk's friend snatched up the binoculars. He pointed them past the bridge to where the road rounded a bend and vanished behind a small hill. From behind that hill rose a big cloud of dust.

"Riders comin' this way, Hawk. Those folk can use more help that just the two of us can give. Here they come round the bend. Great Caesar 's Ghost! Rescue parties don't all wear bandanas over their faces! Hellfire and Damnation! Grab your ammo, Hawk. Head for the gully. This is supposed to be a massacre!"

Blue Hawk reached in his left saddlebag for the box of cartridges for his Winchester rifle. He crammed them into his loose fitting shirt. As he urged his horse forward he saw the man whose real name he did not know leap from the Pinto. A quick step brought him to the coal black stallion's side. As he rode to protect the survivors of the explosion, Blue Hawk knew what would happen next.

The secret knots holding the packages on the black saddle would open with a single yank. In less time than it takes to tell of it the man would tear off his boots and ordinary clothing. From the pack now on the ground came black pants and black boots. A black shirt would follow. Then a black hood that covered all but the eyes. A long black cloak would secure the hood. From another box an all-black double-rig holster set would fly to the man's waist, twin all-black Peacemakers already in place. Finally, a black Stetson completed the change. The unnamed man now had a name known and feared the length and breadth of the west.

Springing into the saddle he would call, "Let's go, Midnight."

And woe to any bandit or dry gulcher riding that day. For The Masked Rider served up Justice from a blazing .45.

Blue Hawk rode as fast as he dared while keeping out of sight of the bridge. At a spot where the gully spread out a bit he urged his mount down to the bottom. A moment later the gully twisted. Several whites came into sight.

A woman tending an injured man saw him and drew back in fright. But then she took in the Yaqui garments he wore. A puzzled look came to her face. This was no local Indian.

"I mean no harm," called out Blue Hawk. The woman only stared at him. Clearly she could not hear what he said. Blue Hawk then gave the open palm sign that meant peace to most people. The woman's face eased.

Seven people sat or lay beyond her. Two men struggled to their feet. Only one succeeded. Blue Hawk reached into his saddlebag for the medical kit. He tossed it to the standing man.

The man caught it. Barely. He looked inside. Understanding dawned.

"Thank you," he said quietly. Then he stepped hesitantly to where a companion lay.

Blue Hawk turned back to the woman. She seemed the most awake of all. He beckoned to her. When she didn't move he repeated the gesture and mouthed the word "please."

He led her to a spot where she could see over the gully wall. He pointed to the bridge and beyond. He ran his fingers across the ground like horses running. He pointed to himself as he assumed a riding position. Then he held up both hands with finders spread. Twice.

"Men coming?" said the women. "Many men?"

Blue Hawk nodded. Then he pulled his collar and shirt front over his mouth and nose. Her eyes went wide.

"Outlaws!?!"

Blue Hawk shrugged, then worked the action of his Winchester. He mouthed the words, "Be ready." He could already hear the approaching horses.

Blue Hawk had his mount lie down. Then he found a forked branch on the gully floor. He appropriated a Stetson to put atop the fork. This he held level with the rim of the gully as the riders thundered across the bridge, leaping the boulders as they came. He moved the hat just a bit.

The woman obviously could not hear the roar of the guns, but she blanched as holes appeared in the hat. He motioned her down as he heard the riders change course. He knew his friend and partner well. In battle they moved and thought almost as one. Any man who looked over the rim was his target. That's where the riders now headed, but not for long. He almost smiled for their coming surprise.

With only the top his head sticking out of a small draw, the Masked Rider tried to count the incoming riders. Clouds of dust made an exact count impossible. Twelve, at least. Maybe fifteen. As the group thundered over the bridge he slipped a sixth round into each Peacemaker and left the guns on half-cock. He finished checking the scabbarded Winchester as the first shots rang out. The gang turned as a whole in the direction of the gully.

"Ride, Midnight!"

The black stallion took off like an arrow from the strongest bow. Reins now in his teeth the Masked Rider guided his mount with his knees. Drowned out by their own horses hoofbeats the owlhoots did not hear him at first.

Then one man saw him charging down on them. He yelled something as he swung his gun hand around. The gun in the Masked Rider's left hand bucked. His target flew backwards out of the kac to land under the next horse's hooves. That mount tumbled forward throwing its rider, adding to the increasing confusion in the gang.

Now his right hand gun spoke. Another man collapsed in the saddle. Still some did not see him. A man dodging the fallen horse looked straight at him.

A scream of pure terror split the noisy air, "The Masked Rider!"

Several owlhoots rounded their horses to find him. A few forgot just how close to the gully they were. Their horses shied from the edge. Gunfire of a different tone cracked from the gully. Three rounds. Three outlaws crumpled.

The Masked Rider heard the first bullet zing past him. Now he opened fire on the concentrated group of rattled outlaws. Right hand. Left hand. Right hand. Horses scattered as their riders gave up control. Left hand. Right hand.

From the middle of the group a strong voice called, "Break off. Head back. Now, dammit!"

Left hand. Right hand. Then the remaining few reached the bridge and the end of accurate pistol range. Slowing to a walk, the Masked Rider holstered his left hand Peacemaker so he could reload the other weapon from his black cartridge belt. His eyes never left the field of battle as he watched for any threat from the fallen.

Blue Hawk made sign to the whites that the enemy had fled. Then he clambered out of the gully. Winchester at the ready he stuffed pistol after pistol from the fallen into his shirt and belt. All the while he checked for signs of life in the would be killers. He found none.

The Masked Rider watched over this grim work. He also swept the whole area for any sign of returning outlaws. He found none. Then Blue Hawk made a pile of weapons near Midnight.

"There are eight alive, Señor," he whispered in Spanish. "Most can not see straight. And none can hear. Only a brown haired woman seems unharmed. I do not think most of them come from here. Maybe from the east."

"Thanks, Hawk. Tell them you saw a single cowboy a couple miles back," replied the Masked Rider in the same language. "Keep helping them until Wade Morgan rides in. Then disappear. Time for me to disappear, right now. Before those looking over the gully rim have to pick up their eyes from the dirt. Follow this party where ever they head, whether Morgan's with them, or not. I'll find you."

"Good luck, Señor," said Blue Hawk, raising a hand. A moment later the Masked Rider and Midnight jumped the boulders on the bridge to vanish from sight.

Blue Hawk could do nothing for those with addled wits. He checked the bandages applied by the white man, then treated a few cuts on that man himself. He feared one older man had a broken leg. A large twisted chunk of metal had fallen on it. He made known that he had seen a single rider on the road before the explosion.

Half an hour later Wade Morgan rode up on the Pinto. Blue Hawk emerged from the gully behind him rifle at the ready.

"Move slowly, hombre," said the Yaqui in English. He was not sure if anyone's hearing had returned.

"What in the Good Lord's name happened here?"

"More like your Devil's name. Whites attacked. Much powder blows up. Then those men come to kill. Blue Hawk and partner fight. Are you friend?"

"I'm not part of that lot of buzzard bait. Iffin that's what you ask. Name's Wade Morgan. Been drifting up from the Yellowstone country. Where be the wagon people?"

"In gully. None can hear me."

"I'll see what I can do for them. Would you do me the favor of roundin' up all those horses? I figure they'll be needed."

Blue Hawk nodded. As he passed Wade Morgan, the waddy whispered, "The riders vamoosed quite a piece." Again the Yaqui nodded.

Wade Morgan vaulted into the gully.

By mid-afternoon Janet Tulane finally felt that things might be coming under control. She no longer constantly fought an urgent sense of panic.

She could hear most things again, plus the ringing in her ears seemed much lower. And help had arrived. First the handsome lone cowboy Morgan rode in and went right to work. Some time later parties from a couple of ranches showed up.

Now all the injured lay under improvised cover with their wounds treated. The cowboys managed to carefully get the lead wagon turned on its side. Now Pops Benson, their camp boss and cook, directed the salvage of their remaining gear. The crusty old fellow sat on a boulder with his splinted leg on a smaller rock. Since a number of the cowboys knew him, a spirited dialog flew back and forth about his sitting under her bright red parasol for protection from the sun.

Janet looked around as she barely heard a wagon rolling up. It was the buckboard one group of cowboys brought. That meant the dead gunmen were now laid out in the town four miles to the south. The Sheriff of that town rode in with the buckboard.

Sheriff Henry Wilson had been a lawman in the west most of the time since the Civil War ended. He thought he'd seen about everything when it came to strange parties from the east. But he definitely had not seen a new crater anywhere near the size of this one since the War. Pulling a tablet of paper from his saddlebag the Sheriff ambled over to where a comely young woman sat watching over six men stretched out on the ground. A couple of the men looked him over as he approached. The rest seemed dazed.

"'Scuse me, ma'am, I'm Sheriff Wilson of the town you camped near last night. Who's in charge of your party?"

"That would be Professor Halbert M. Tulane, Sheriff. I'm his daughter, Janet. We think he is mildly concussed. Matter of fact, everybody, except for me and Pops Benson, doesn't feel up to much right now. I'll try to answer any questions."

"Thank you, Miss Tulane. Why do you think the two of you are better off than the others?"

"My father and Herb Dover both threw themselves on top of me right before the blast. The last thing I saw was Pops getting set. After he unhooked his team, he grabbed his bag of sourdough starter from the wagon boot. He rolled into the gully and wrapped the bag around his head. But most of our centrifuge landed on his leg, so I'm the only one really walking."

"Every blessed one of you's lucky to even be alive," said the Sheriff. "Now please tell me who everybody is. You didn't lose anybody. Did you?"

"Maybe we don't feel very lucky, but I've said a prayer of thanks. Everybody is alive. Next to me is my father. He's a paleontologist. Like the others, he's from the University of New Hampshire. Over there's Dr. Raymond Quincy Trevor. He's a PhD. type of doctor, a geologist. Herb is Hubert Randall Dover, the Third. He's a graduate student in both geology and paleontology. Pops Benson, well, I don't know what his full name is."

"Nobody does," chuckled Wilson. "Some say he started out as a Mountain Man. I've known him for a long time. Known those last three for a piece, too. Lou, Mart, and Sam Zachery been round these parts many a year. Good men, all.

"Now, would you be so kind as to tell me the reason y'all came out here. People in these parts hear geologist they think a prospecting for gold. Don't want any wild talk startin' a rush of any kind."

"I hadn't thought about that, Sheriff," laughed Janet. As she looked over the lawman's shoulder she noticed Wade Morgan examining the mostly demolished side of one of the rear wagons. "This is strictly a paleontology expedition. Uncle Ray, that's honorary Uncle, came along because he wants to see this part of the west. And, the two fields are directly related, you know."

"Can't say that I did," replied Wilson. "Read an article in *Harper's Weekly* about finding the remains of shellfish turned to rock. And found in places that don't seem right for 'um. Is that what your father looks into?"

"That's one part of it, Sheriff. There's a theory that the whole Missouri River basin, a long long time ago, was part of an inland sea. Like the Great Salt Lake, only bigger than Texas, and then some. At about the same time, some scientists think that Devils Tower was even with the surrounding ground. We want to test both theories. We're slated to spend the next six weeks about four miles west of Devils Tower where rainwater has exposed a fifteen yard high wall rich in fossils. That might keep us busy until we have to return east. If not we might take a closer look at the Tower in August."

"Six weeks a lookin' at a wall of rocks. Now that's got my poor head spinning," replied Sheriff Wilson. "Better get back to the here and now. Anything strange happened before today?"

Before she began to speak Janet noticed Wade Morgan now stood just a few feet away. "A couple of things, Sheriff. My father, using the University's banker, arranged for a ten-thousand dollar line-of-credit with a major bank out here. When we got to the railhead they told us it had been cancelled.

...she noticed Wade Morgan
examining the rear wagons.

That took three days to straighten out. By then our outfitter cancelled the order we wired ahead for. Took another two days to put together what we needed. And there seemed like nobody had any explosives on hand. Luckily we found this mining company that just went bust. To get any explosives we had to take their entire stock. About ten times what we really wanted. But that was the only deal in town. So we hired Pappy and the Zachery's. They put our little wagon train together. We got started over a week late. With the explosives we couldn't do much about making up time.

"This morning we passed through your town. Later we came down that last hill. Pappy saw the boulders at this end of the bridge. He stopped us a ways from the bridge. In case of bandits under the bridge, he said. Next thing I knew the air was full of flaming arrows. At least two of them hit the sides and cargo tarpaulins of every wagon. Then came some war-hoops and some Indians, I guess they were Indians, galloped away from here in the gully.

"We tried to put the arrows out. But we couldn't. So Pappy and the others told us to head for the gully while they let the horses loose. With the horses running away, the last thing I saw over the rim was Pappy grabbing that bag of sourdough. Then Daddy tackled me and Herb piled on top of both of us a moment later. Then things went dark.

"Sometime later I got out from under them and saw what had happened. I tried to help the others. Then this Indian rode up. He gave us a medical kit and warned me about bandits coming in. All by sign. I couldn't hear a thing. Then the gun battle happened. I know the Indian only fired three shots. A little later help started arriving. I think you know the rest."

"Why weren't you scared by this particular Indian, ma'am?"

"Pops Benson told us a lot about the local tribes. Only he called them 'peoples.' Described how they tend to dress and act. The Indian that helped us wore a Mexican sombrero, or something like one."

"That's no local Indian I've ever heard of," exclaimed Sheriff Wilson. "Can you describe the Indians in the gully, Miss Tulane"

"Not well. They wore no shirts, had long hair, with feathers of some kind. Rode without any saddle I could see. I only saw them for a second. Then we tended to the wagons."

"Sheriff," came a strong new voice, "I think I can help a piece, here. I looked hard. There ain't been an unshod pony in the gully for many a day. Probably since the last big rain. And, here be the heads of three of them fire arrows. Most disappeared in the blast. I dug these outta the end wagons."

With that the man placed three things in the Sheriff's outstretched hand.

"Target arrows!" growled Wilson. "Wrapped with rope. Probably with the ends frayed open ta burn faster."

"Spread the rope a bit. Smells like coal oil." said the newcomer.

"A frame up. White snakes playing Indian. Thanks, compadre. I don't think I caught your name."

"Didn't throw it. Wade Morgan's my handle. Been driftin' north. Got here 'bout half an hour after ta blast."

The third day after the blast Barton Link sat in his office two doors down from the Queen of the Black Hills saloon in the town of Carter's Rock. He studied the best survey map available for the territory to the north. He penciled a note on the lands owned by the Circle-Z ranch. An amount of money to buy the owner out if the big project got delayed. Shadings in red pencil indicated the area he already controlled. He tried to decide whether to try to replace the men he had recently lost when his office door slammed open. He held his angry tongue as he realized Big George Filstrap, his right hand man seemed clearly worried.

"Boss, we got a problem!" gasped Big George. "Th' perrfesser's gone. Cinda-May took up his grub an' he jumped her. Took her dress, shoes, and that big bonnet she likes. Went down the stairs an' right to the outhouse wearing 'em. Nobody's seen him, or her since! Got some of the boys lookin' through town. And nobody's yellin' about missing a mount."

Link spat out a livid phrase or two. Then he began giving orders that Professor Reginald Turnbull be found and returned immediately. Alive, preferably. Dead, if necessary. With no evidence left for others to find.

The man using the name Professor Reginald Turnbull scuttled across the the grass and scrub headed northwest, he hoped, from Carter's Rock. Now he worried about being found. Or stepping on a rattlesnake. Or something. Not that he'd been treated badly these last three weeks. A reasonable amount of spirits. All he wanted to eat. Even passing time with the saloon girls who brought him his meals.

Still, the old adage proved true. A velvet lined cage was still a cage. And, if he stayed long enough, Link would probably stake him out for the buzzards. He was sorry he ever met Barton Link. It seemed so simple. Get hold of some of the man's excess funds before disappearing over the horizon. He'd sold this bait three times before. And he had enough "salt" for that many more. But Link proved to be a wary fellow. And he saw potential enemies behind every bush.

Once hooked, Link made plans of a scope beyond belief. Started asking questions that had "Professor Turnbull" taking wild guesses and generally inventing things out of whole cloth. The bad part was that Link understood just enough about rocks and minerals not to swallow any old fairy tale.

The "Professor" headed in the one direction he believed Link would not look for him. At least not at first. All the talk he'd overheard about the scientific expedition. How they almost got blown to Kingdom Come. How lawmen, honest lawmen, took an interest. Maybe even rode with them. His only chance might be to throw himself on the mercy of the law. The Sheriff in Carter's Rock was said to be honest enough. But he and the lawman would have been dead before the Sheriff could get him out of town. Much less to someplace safe.

So the "Professor" stumbled ahead in hopes of finding the scientific party with enough firepower to turn back the band of murderous range scum soon to be out for his blood. Their guard force could protect him. He just needed a little bit of luck for the next few hours.

At that same time the "guard force" of Professor Tulane's expedition consisted of Wade Morgan and the still slightly shaky Zachery brothers. Reassured by various letters of identification and credit that Tulane always carried on his person, Sheriff Wilson helped re-outfit the party with as much as his town of Fortier Flats could provide. Wilson had identified one of the dead as McBirth Williams, leader of a gang of cut-throat outlaws. Whatever Williams' purpose for the raid, the danger died with him, Wilson reasoned. Wade Morgan was not so sure. Williams had been one of the first to fall, but the attack continued.

Morgan allowed himself to be talked into signing on with the party. The day following the blast four wagons headed once more for Devil's Tower. Morgan drove lead. Pops Benson drove tail, with the energetic Uncle Ray Trevor providing assistance if he faltered. One of the Zachery's and young Herb Dover teamed up, with the other two brothers spelling each other in the fourth wagon. A few of the local cowboys rode with them until the trail branched for their spreads. Calling their heartfelt thanks the Tulane party headed for an area about four miles west of Devils Tower.

Blue Hawk, Wade Morgan knew, glided somewhere near the wagons, as quiet as his namesake. Morgan wanted a parlay. A few things he picked up from the friendly cow punchers worried him. Several spreads relatively near the Tower stood empty. Some bought out. Some said to have gone under. But chimney smoke could be seen rising from the ranch buildings. And wagon tracks were spotted headed from a town called Carter's Rock in the general direction of those spreads in recent days. Morgan sat uneasy in the saddle wanting to scout these "abandoned" ranches.

About noon they passed the fork in the road leading to Carter's Rock. A small sign told them that grub, supplies, and the Queen of the Black Hills saloon waited for them about just a mile and a half in that direction. That close to their line of travel, Morgan suggested that he check out the place for getting supplied after the party got settled in. Believing Sheriff Wilson's conclusion about their safety, the Professor agreed.

They found a good camp location in the late afternoon. With everything set up Pops Benson and Janet Tulane began a lively "discussion" about who should prepare dinner. This entertained the rest of the party until enchiladas, made with beans and pork, hit their plates. Wade Morgan volunteered to walk the camp parameter for the whole night.

Morgan woke about noon the following day. He found the camp fully established. Janet Tulane directed the Zachery brothers in the setting up of what scientific equipment that had survived, or had been replaced. The three academics already prowled the "wall of rock" trying to decide where to begin digging for fossilized pay dirt.

Before he headed for Carter's rock the following afternoon Wade Morgan circled the camp looking for potential problems. About half way around a twig snapped near him. Morgan whistled a couple of notes.

"Here, Señor," came a low whisper in Spanish to his right.

"Any problems for the camp?" replied Morgan in a similar voice.

"No, Señor, not for more than a mile."

"I'm headed for Carter's Rock down that branch road back a piece. Might stir some trouble. Cover me."

Dusk came as Wade Morgan rode into the town of Carter's Rock. He let the pinto keep to a slow walk as he took in the sights. The town took the form of a capital letter "T". Morgan rode from the bottom of the letter's upright to the top. He passed a number of businesses. Some few had living space above the stores. Some right behind. And a handful of dwellings stood off a ways.

He took note of the blacksmith and livery, the tiny barbershop that also seemed to offer dental work. And the Dry Goods Store two doors down from a large General Store. Then he came to the letter's crossbar. And that part of town could not have been better described. For both the corner buildings were large two story saloons. The Copper Penny on the left. The Queen of the Black Hills on the right. Through the ground floor windows he could see both drinking establishments did slow business. As a couple of lights were lit, the shadows on the second floor window shades of the Queen told him about other business being conducted.

Then a man emerged from the building dead ahead. He carried two lit kerosene lanterns. He used a hooked pole to place one at each end of a sign on the second floor balcony. Now Morgan read that this was the "Carter's Rock Temple of God."

To the left he took note of a sign marking the office of the Sheriff. Morgan turned right and hitched the Pinto in front of a window with a roughly painted notice that this was the Law Office of Obidiah Clampett. A paper sign below further revealed, "Out Prospecting - Back Monday."

"My kind of lawyer," Morgan told himself as he headed to the saloon called The Copper Penny.

He stood in the bat-wing doors for just a moment getting the lay of the place. This being Wednesday night just about everybody here must be from in town. He stepped inside casually, not wanting to draw anymore attention than necessary for a strange face. The Wheel of Fortune had a cover over it. Five men seemed to be having a penny ante game of stud poker going to the left. To his right four men with fresh glasses of beer played either Bridge, or maybe Whist.

Morgan ambled up to the bar. He counted a dozen different types of Whiskey and ten more of other spirits in bottles behind the bar. The bartender looked pretty bored, but he put on an attentive face as he approached.

"Evening stranger. What'll you have?"

Morgan put a half dollar on the bar. "Ya have any wine?"

The fellow perked up a bit. "Got a shipment from the Stone Hill outfit in Hermann, Missouri, a couple weeks ago. Got a preference?"

"I hear their plain red's pretty good."

"So I'm told. Long as you don't mind it in a beer glass."

"Long as you serve it in a clean beer glass."

"Deal!" smiled the bartender.

"Just the townies tonight?" asked Morgan as he took his first sip.

"You bet. And you. You lookin' for work?"

"Got some. Starts tomorrow. Some college people from the east. Wanta prove this dried out piece of Wyoming used to be an ocean."

"I heard about them birds. Had a bad accident day before yesterday. Hell, the whole blame territory heard the blast. You musta heard it."

"Heard it," laughed Morgan. "'Bout got knocked off my horse by it. Helped 'em pick up what pieces worth pickin' up. Got hired on. Headin' to their camp tomorrow. Say, this be some fine wine. You tried it?"

"Only sniffed it, friend. I took the pledge two years ago. An' I haven't broken it."

"You're a brave man," chuckled Morgan. "A workin' here in the midst of all this temptation."

Morgan then queried the man about the local stores, the smithy, and other services the Tulane Party might need. He received what he took to be straight answers.

With the business part of the visit about over Morgan took another sip of the wine. He almost strangled on it as a strident set of musical notes split the evening air. He coughed a bit before exclaiming, "What in the name of Sam Hill's that?"

"That, friend, is the Reverend Mister Ellis Throneberry a-gettin' warmed up. Nobody knows how, or why, but Brother Throneberry totes a genuine steam calliope around with him. Gives a short concert every night 'bout now. Hopes everyone 'll come listen to him preach for a few minutes."

By now the strains of the hymn Amazing Grace made conversation difficult. "How long does he keep at it?" said Morgan in a louder voice.

"Thanking Heaven for small favors, he's only got a small boiler for the contraption. One more hymn and she'll be dry. But, ifin he doesn't get a crowd, he fills the thing up again. If you bring back the glass, feel free to go out and listen."

Over the opening bars of Rock of Ages Morgan said, "Thanks, Barkeep. Think I will."

Wade Morgan sauntered out onto the saloon's boardwalk, glass in hand. Shortly after the last note faded away a tall gangly man emerged from from one of the sets of doors in the front of the Carter's Rock Temple of God. Dressed in black with a clerical collar, he shoved a wood pulpit to the edge of the boardwalk. A few of the people gathered in the streets themselves and on the boardwalks of the two saloons called out to him. Genuine seeming greetings mixed with a few cat-calls.

The Reverend Mr. Throneberry took all that in stride. He called a return greeting, then announced the birth of a baby boy to the Johnston family. With that he launched into an emotional indictment of various forms of sin punctuated by Bible verse. Here he sounded just about like any stump preacher Wade Morgan could remember. Then the topic changed.

"Friends, whether you heed my other warnings, remember this. Steer clear of that abomination known as The Devil's Tower. For you could loose your very soul to the worst enemy of all things good and pure. Stay away from that evil place..."

Mr. Throneberry continued in that vein as Wade Morgan finished his wine, returned the glass, and disappeared between the buildings.

Ellis Throneberry lit the pile of wood in the middle of the street in front of the Temple of God with a splash of coal oil. He shoved his rolling pulpit to the back side of the boardwalk before entering the Temple. A cowboy seated on one of the benches facing the church's alter startled him. He'd seen nobody come in. And he kept the back door locked. The man's face would be considered handsome by most women he decided. His outfit seemed well worn, including his six-gun and holster. Throneberry had never seen the man before. He was sure of it.

"Good evening, Pilgrim," he said. "How can a humble servant of God help you?"

"Actually, Preacher," drawled Wade Morgan, "I thought I might be able to help you."

That took Ellis Throneberry aback. He turned to straighten one of the benches before sitting to face the cowboy. "Help me how, my friend?"

"Heard you haranguing the people tonight. 'Bout sin, and lust, and all the things set out in the Ten Commandments. All that's fine and good. An' you picked a whale of a spot to do it from."

When the cowboy paused, the preacher smiled, "Why thank you, Pilgrim. But, I think you have something else to say I won't like as much."

"Didn't want to say anything in front of the crowd when you called the Tower the home of Ol' Scratch himself. Told people to stay away from it. Whites might be wise to keep their distance, but not 'cause of Lucifer."

Throneberry felt a knot forming in his stomach. What did this cowboy know? "What better reason than the Devil?" he asked.

"Devil's got nothin' to do with it, Preacher. That's a myth got started by a bad translation. Mosta the Indian tribes in this whole region tell stories 'bout a giant bear living there. The place is sacred to the Lakota Sioux, Cheyenne and Kiowa, just to name three peoples. That's enough for whites to be wary of the place. Indians call that hunk a rock things like Bear's Tipi an' Bear's Lodge Butte.

"Anyways, Colonel Dodge's survey party came through. And his fool translator said the Indians called the place 'The Bad God's Tower.' That got made into Devil's Tower. Ain't nobody, white or Indian, ever said the place was evil, or claimed by Satan. Leastwise, I never heard 'bout anything like that 'till tonight. Didn't want to bring it up in front of the sinners you're trying so hard to save. Thought I speak private with you."

"I thank you, Pilgrim. Will you be staying on here in Carter's Rock?"

"I'll be in an' out. My new job'll get me in now and then."

Wade Morgan walked out the front of the Carter's Rock Temple of God. He looked up and down the both the town's streets. Then he sauntered over to the Queen of the Black Hills saloon. The place seemed almost deserted. No townies here. Just a small stakes poker game, three cowboys chewing the fat, and a couple of solitary drinkers.

Morgan ordered a beer at the bar. The bartender told him they closed in about half an hour. Morgan nursed his beer standing at the bar. All the while he watched his back with the big mirrors on the wall.

A few minutes later a weasel faced man scuttled in. He stopped at the poker game for a moment, then joined the three talkers. The poker game broke up with the end of the next hand. The men drifted out to the street.

Five minutes later Wade Morgan reluctantly left most of his good beer on the bar and headed for his horse. As he stepped into the darkened street he made sure his Colt rode loose in its holster. Some instinct told him trouble lay in his immediate future.

As he approached his horse a voice came from the shadows between the buildings.

"Hey, saddle tramp. Hear you've been a raising Cain with our poor Preacher."

Morgan slowed. He didn't look around, but his ears caught some slight sound of movement on the boardwalk on the other side of the street.

The voice came again, "You answer when you're spoken to, saddle tramp."

Morgan stopped. "Be good to see ifin somebody's really a-talkin', or am I jus' hearin' gusts of wind." Now supposedly quiet footsteps ground their way across the graveled street.

A second somebody drew breath in the space next to the Lawyers office. But the same voice came again.

"The Preacher don't need no saddle tramp puttin' wild ideas in his head. You got that?"

"That's fer the Preacher to decide, friend. Not someone 'fraid to show his face!"

The feet stopped advancing not too far behind him. A shadow detached itself from darkness to step onto the boardwalk. Starlight and the lone wood street fire in front of the Temple defined a burley man in rough clothing with a double rig gun belt. A hand quivered above each gun butt.

Wade Morgan dropped into a deep crouch. His left hand swept the street picking up dust and gravel. Before the gunslinger in front of him could react Morgan took one crab-like step to the side. He spun around flinging the handful of street debris in a high wide arc behind him. Coughing and curses erupted from that direction.

Now his Colt leapt into his hand as his eyes returned to the other direction. The gunfighter was finishing his draw. Morgan began to work the trigger, going for the man's shoulder.

He never finished his shot. A rock sailed out of the darkness to impact above the fellow's ear. He fell twitching like a wrung neck chicken.

Gun still in hand Morgan spun around. Two shadows behind him still dug at their faces trying to clear their eyes. He stepped quickly forward. His left fist sank wrist deep into the pudgy stomach of the first man. Then he clipped the other's head with the butt of the Colt. Back in a crouch he readied himself to fire into the small space between the buildings.

The call of a prairie chicken sounded above the lawyer's window. At the same time came a bellow of "What the Hell goes on there!?" from the other end of the T's top street.

"Who be you?" replied Morgan.

"Red Chambers, the Sheriff!" came the call as a lean figure trotted past the street fire. "Holster your guns, ifin they be out, or else!"

Morgan slipped his Colt back into its holster. "Don't want no grief, Sheriff."

A moment later the Sheriff slowed to a walk. He took in the scene with

"...he clipped the other's head
with the butt of his Colt."

an old Confederate Cavalry pistol rock steady in his big fist. "Two out cold. An' one coughin' his guts up. That leaves jus' you to explain things, stranger. Who be **you?** An' what went on?"

"Name's Morgan. Wade Morgan. Jus' rode in tonight ta see the sights. An ta wet my tonsils. Had a chat with the preacher, then spent a little time at the Queen. Went for my horse when that fella called me out fer talkin' to the good Mr. Throneberry. Got downright insultin'. Meanwhile those two lead footed hombres tried ta bushwhack me from behind. That rock hadn'ta worked I was fixin' ta shoot the loudmouth."

The Sheriff turned the gunslinger over with his boot. Then he whistled. "Grover Adams. Hired gun. Not the best, Morgan, but you were real good. Or real lucky. Been better for you ifin you plugged him. Watch your back. He's the kind what shoots from that direction. All three work for Barton Link. Link came from back east a prospector. Never found no gold or silver. But he might as well mint the stuff when he figured out how to remove it from other folks. He owns the Queen. Wants ta own the whole town. Hell, he even bought out a couple of ranches up towards Devil's Tower. If your jus' passin' through, might be better if you vamoosed. Less you want to press charges. Then there'll be at least five people we can't see now who'll swear on Throneberry's best Bible they saw you start this fracas."

"Sounds like a fine idea to me, Sheriff. I'll be on my way. Say, is that hawg-leg th' nine-shooter with the buckshot chaser?"

"That is is. Took it off a dead Reb officer at Chickasaw Mountain. Pain in th' rump to load. Have ta cast my own slugs. But it gets th' job done, an' a heap o' respect."

"Don't doubt that, Sheriff," drawled Morgan as he mounted. "Good night to ya. An' thanks for listening ta' a stranger."

Morgan headed out of Carter's Rock by the shortest way possible. Then he swung his mount in the direction of the scientist's camp. About two miles later another rider fell in beside him.

"No one follows, Señor."

"Nice pitch with that rock, Hawk. Gunplay would've caused more problems."

"One more hid between the buildings. Was like a whiff of smoke. Gone when the gunman went down."

"I thought there might be one more. But now we've got the name of one enemy. Barton Link. Not sure why, but I want to know more about him."

Ellis Throneberry rose before dawn, as was his custom. He dressed and ate the last of the berries he'd picked on his previous morning's outing. As he left the back of his church he could hear people tending to chickens and cows. In the distance the blacksmith's bellows coaxed the forge fire ever hotter.

Throneberry hurried to lose the sounds of civilization. He walked more than a mile to where he had staked a private claim on a plot of land. Here stood two benches. One under a lean to shelter. The other in the open air. The false dawn that romantics called the Belt of Venus turned the eastern horizon purple as he sat down on the uncovered bench. He remembered the first time he'd left the squalid tenements of New York City. The first time he experienced the dawn without buildings obstructing the view. God's Dawn he called it.

Now he hummed as he waited. Sometimes hymns. Sometimes popular or patriotic songs. He watched the few clouds change from gray and black to flaming red and orange. He felt alive again. And, he hoped, closer to God. A smile on his face, he studied the sunrise in its glory until the sky became the blue of the day.

Then he fell to his knees and clasped his hands in prayer. He prayed for wisdom. He prayed for guidance. Tears fell from his eyes to the ground at his knees. His voice shook as he said aloud, "The path, Lord. Please show me the path!" He knelt there a moment more. Then he rose and stretched. As he rubbed his eyes a powerful voice came from behind him.

"I can show you one path, Parson. The path of Justice."

Ellis Throneberry spun around. Had his prayers been answered? Behind him stood a tall man dressed all in black. A black hood covered all his face save his piercing eyes. The black cloak on his shoulders gave him the form Ellis imagined a Western Angel of Death would take. He reeled. A strong hand fell on his shoulder."

"Sit, Parson. Before you fall down. I did not mean to frighten you. At least not that much. I am no Angel. Or Devil, for that matter. I think of myself as a Top Hand for Justice. Do you understand me?"

Now seated firmly on the bench of his own making Ellis Throneberry gathered his courage. Finally he said, "I think I understand. Are you the Masked Rider?"

"Some call me that. Others call me things I won't repeat to a man of God. You are a real man of God, so I hear. But something has got you all twisted up inside. Wouldn't surprise me if that had something to do with Barton Link. He seems to take a hand in just about everyone's game, invited, or not."

"Indeed he does" spat Throneberry. "He arranged for me to get in a situation with one of his saloon girls. Miss Phoenix is the name she uses. She'd asked me questions about God's Love and His Forgiveness a time or two when we met on the streets. Sincere questions, I thought. Then she asked to meet me at the church. She seemed very unhappy about something. She came in all tense like that evening. I asked her over to the corner where I have my desk. By the time I finished sitting down and turning back to her she'd managed to loose most of her clothing. Afore I could tell her to put everything back on Link and his tame storekeeper rushed in."

"Parson, you were set up, right and proper," growled the Masked Rider.

"Indeed I was," replied Throneberry. "And I think Miss Phoenix was too. She started to cry a river. I think she started to say she was sorry, but Link told her to be quiet."

"So, suddenly you were in Link's pocket."

"Still am, if the sinner ever lets it get about. He didn't want much. He even wanted me to continue my evening sermons on the boardwalk. So long as I only talked about Sin in real general terms. Later he 'suggested' I start going on about how evil Devils Tower was. That seemed harmless enough until that cowboy told me how that name came about."

If a man could look pensive while wearing a mask, Ellis decided that the Masked Rider did for the next moment or two. Then the Robin Hood outlaw began asking questions about the town. And about Barton Link's operations.

When he finished the sun highlighted the man's Stetson and cloak. He threw back the cloak to reveal the black gun belt with twin black Colts.

"Parson, will you help me clean up this mess? I'm not asking for you to fight. Or lie. Just listen, and give out any information I need spread."

"Anything within the law," Ellis Throneberry heard himself say. "How will I know...?"

The Masked Rider picked up a stick. He traced a strangely bent cross on the ground. "That's an Indian sign for good luck, Parson. Anything, or anybody I send to you will wear that sign, or make it. If anyone happened to see us together, just say that I scared the curds and whey out of you. And told you not to say anything."

"That's close enough to the truth," chuckled Ellis Throneberry grimly.

Then the Masked Rider was gone.

Late the following night "Professor Turnbull" stumbled along through the darkness. A true tenderfoot, he worried about those tender feet to the exclusion of almost everything else. He did not notice the area of the sky to the right of his course completely devoid of stars. He simply blundered ahead in what he hoped was the right direction.

Then the moon rose. His oblivion to his surroundings vanished. For the moon illuminated the face of Devils Tower in bright light and inky shadows. And he was less that two miles away. Turnbull could not calculate that distance with any accuracy, but his heart dropped like a stone. The Tower was far too close. Barton Link's hired outlaws patrolled all around the huge landmark. Link himself told him so.

Panic turned Turnbull about ninety degrees to his left and gave him the energy to run like Lucifer nipped at his heels. For about three hundred yards he sprinted through the night. Brush tore at his clothes. At his flesh. He tripped over a rock to go sprawling next to a nest of Prairie Chickens. The nesting pair flew at his face to protect their eggs. He changed direction again to avoid them.

When he could no longer run, he walked. When he could no longer walk, he staggered. When he could no longer stagger, he fell motionless to the ground. His adrenalin exhausted, he passed out. But his wild rush had sewn seeds of his doom.

Not twenty minutes after dawn Lacrosse Randall, a Canadian on the run from the Northwest Mounted Police, rode his last circuit of night guard for Devil's Tower. His area covered much of the southwest quadrant around the impressive pile of rocks. Hungry enough to eat a lizard, Randall hoped for an early relief. Late comers to the table got slim pickings. He felt his mouth water with hunger as he crested a low hill.

Then he got a look at the path ahead. He swore to himself as he dismounted. His Dragoon .44 pistol in hand, he scanned the area. Advancing he squinted at the tracks that cut across his area of responsibility. An hour ago, even with the moonlight, the markings had been invisible. Little chow for him. Ignoring sign like this was a good way to get shot by his employer. A moment later Randall remounted his horse to begin following Professor Turnbull's almost drunken seeming trail.

Wade Morgan's bedroll stretched out under a canvas tarp on the edge of the University of Connecticut camp. Even asleep the man's finely honed senses would catch anything out of place. A tiny pebble sailed in from the brush. It glanced off the sleeping man's left hand. Fully awake before he opened one eye, Morgan knew the source. Only the Yaqui could get that close without disturbing him.

Certain sounds mixed into the pre-dawn silence. Morgan quietly rose. He strapped on his gun belt before heading out of camp like a man heeding the call of nature. In a nearby wash Blue Hawk greeted him.

"A man comes toward the camp, Señor. He walks like he is drunk. More noise almost than a fiesta. This way."

Morgan fell in behind the Yaqui. Silently they hurried in the direction of Devils Tower. Soon both heard sounds of a man stumbling through brush a sane man would walk around. Then Morgan picked up another sound. "Was that a horse?" he hissed.

"I heard none before," said Blue Hawk as they looked over the rim of an arroyo.

An older man in the shreds of a fancy set of clothes made his uncertain way in their general direction. His feet were stuffed into a pair of fancy women's shoes. One glance at the face told the story. Total exhaustion.

Morgan gathered himself to offer assistance. Then the loop of a lariat sailed up from behind the man. The rope settled expertly over his shoulders. Then the rope's owner yanked cruelly back, just as hard as he could. Professor Reginald Turnbull's spent body flew backwards. His head glanced off a rock nearly buried in the ground.

From the other end of the rope came a string of curses in French, followed by, "Got you! Be glad I am not a cannibal. I missed my breakfast chasin' you. I should roast you over a spit." The diatribe stopped as Randall realized Turnbull's condition. "Merry Hades! Now I've got to carry you!!"

In the arroyo Wade Morgan motioned Blue Hawk to one side and gave one other very clear sign. Then he stepped to level ground.

"I don't think you'll get far. Just leave him here."

Lacrosse Randall blanched. "Nobody tells me what to do," he growled as his hand streaked to his six-gun.

Wade Morgan stood still, as if nothing was the matter. Before the hogleg finished clearing leather Blue Hawk's boot knife spun across the scrub and stopped hilt deep into Randall's chest.

A moment later Morgan said, "Hit his head pretty bad. I'll carry him to camp. You backtrack, Hawk. Change his tracks into some other direction.

And dump this polecat where he won't be found a spell."

Blue Hawk nodded. Pausing only to take the ladies slippers he headed back towards Devils Tower.

"Professor, have you got any idea what these might be?" Morgan said as he rolled some clay crusted stones from his hand onto the improvised work table.

Professor Tulane put down the ancient shellfish he'd been examining. He glanced at the stones. Then he scraped a bit of clay off of one with his pen-knife. Putting the clay under his lens, he studied the sample.

"Not like any kind of soil we've catalogued here, Mr. Morgan," he finally stated. "Where did you find them?"

"On the injured man, sir. Since he can't rightly talk, I decided to have a close look at his outfit. Seems the feller had these sewn inta the padded shoulders of his coat. Some papers, too. Filled the extra space cotton wool so's nothing rattled."

"That is strange indeed. Why don't you show them to Dr. Trevor. That's his professional field, after all."

Wade Morgan found Trevor jawing with the Zachery brothers. The three seemed to be taking turns telling an extremely tall tale. Trevor wrote furiously in a large notebook.

The tale concluded, Morgan spoke up, "Dr. Trevor, could you spare me a moment?"

"Of course, Mr. Morgan. Thank you, friends. We'll pick this up again sometime."

Alone with the academic, Morgan said, "I hope you don't take that yarn seriously."

"Of course not. Strange as it sounds, I'm doing research on western legends."

"That does sound a tad strange from a Geologist, and not an English Professor," replied Morgan dubiously.

"Mr. Morgan, can you keep a harmless personal secret?"

"I know how to keep my mouth shut."

"Very well, then. I teach at one of the nation's best universities. But I make about the same amount of money as a writer of Dime Novels. Don't laugh, my friend, its true. I've written Secret Service with the King Bradys; plus Frank Reade, Junior; Buffalo Bill; and even Deadwood Dick's adventures without ever being west of the Mississippi. That's one reason I came along. To gather material. The more outrageous the better. Now how can I help you?"

Wade Morgan chewed over what he'd just heard. He hoped the topic of the Masked Rider would not come up. "I found these on the injured man. Can you tell me what they are?"

A short time later Dr. Trevor gave his opinion. Wade Morgan's head spun with the news. And a whole bunch of new puzzle pieces came into play.

Morgan and Trevor quickly returned to the tent where the mysterious man lay. They found Janet Tulane cleaning the fellow up. A further search of his clothing produced nothing useful.

Then, at Janet's touch with a cool wet cloth the man began to mumble. "Crazy... He's crazy. Won't placer. Wants mother... Wants it all... All's not there..."

The three exchanged puzzled looks at the words. Then Janet pressed his thick beard flat with her wash cloth. The trio realized the man had a severely receding chin.

Something clicked in Wade Morgan's head. Quickly he opened the man's shirt to reveal the right shoulder. His action exposed a Confederate Army tattoo. Morgan said something unpleasant in the Yaqui tongue.

"Thunderation!" he continued. "That's Chinless Smithers. Guess he took somebody what didn't like it."

"Took somebody?" said Janet. "What do you mean?"

"Don't know the Easterner's name for it, but I reckon Dr. Trevor does," replied Morgan winking at the academic. "If I set foot in New York City somebody like Smithers would sell me that big bridge they built to Brooklyn City."

"You mean a 'confidence man,'" laughed Janet. "Don't be surprised, Mr. Morgan. I transcribe all of Uncle Ray's manuscripts into something his editors can read. Now, I think we'd better talk to my father."

"Professor," said Wade Morgan, "last I heard Chinless Smithers was a selling shares in fake gold mines and such. His mumbling fits that. Looks like he just changed the pay dirt, but not the game. Now he's selling diamond mines, 'ccording to Dr. Trevor. I'm a betting he hooked somebody way too strong for him. His victim swallowed the bait, an' the whole fishing pole, to boot. Now Smithers' runnin' afore the scheme falls apart. By his tracks he came from the direction of Devils Tower. Good thing your party ain't headed there till next month. And a lot of people know that. With your permission I want to get my eyes up close on the Tower. Bet I'll find something plumb interesting..."

Blue Hawk handed the binoculars to his friend dressed as Wade Morgan. But the Yaqui knew that Morgan was not the name his friend came into the world to. He did not know the Masked Rider's true name. Nor did he really want to. But, sometimes he wondered exactly what upbringing led to his long, seemingly endless campaign, to rid the west of outlaws and killers. Not just in the lands of the United States, for Blue Hawk had helped and been hunted by the Scarlet Riders of the north and the Federales of his native Mexico. The Masked Rider's justice knew not borders.

"Scan the lip of the Tower," said Blue Hawk in Spanish. The man currently called Wade Morgan took a long look.

"Thunderation! That looks like wood framing. Must overhang the edge fifty feet. I never heard tell of Devils Tower being climbed."

"It has been now, Señor. But why?"

"I'd give a bunch to be able to answer that, Hawk. Wait... Wait... Concarn it! The thing's being pulled in. Can't see it at all now. We're just lucky you spotted the thing in the first place. That means there's a party living on top of the Tower.

"But why? Somebody's paying plenty. Keeping at least one gang of cold blooded riders ready to massacre for no apparent reason. That is until Chinless Smithers turned up. Arranged not just to climb Devils Tower, but to haul up maybe a couple tons of logs and gear to the top. Some folks would try to climb the thing just for the thrill of doing it. But why in the world build up there? They planning to winch people up for the view? Laugh if you want, Hawk. Some people would pay two bits for the privilege. But they hide the darn rig. That's got trouble written all over, right there."

Late that afternoon, as the shadows began to lengthen, Wade Morgan and Blue Hawk eased their way over the crest of a small hill about a quarter mile from Devils Tower. Each carried a bundle of fresh cut brush and leaves. Lying down among some tall brush they covered themselves with the material. Wade Morgan checked some landmarks on Devils Tower to assure himself that their position almost directly faced the log construction twelve-hundred feet above.

They settled in to wait. Sounds came to them. Sounds of horses and wagons. Sounds of men's voices almost too faint to hear. The sound of axes on wood punctuated everything else. Invisible in the trees surrounding the Tower lay a work camp of some kind. A set of wagon ruts broke the turf about a hundred yards in front of them. Morgan scanned that trail with his binoculars. Used to seeing knee deep wagon ruts from huge Conestoga prairie schooners, these much smaller ones looked strange. Then Blue Hawk touched his arm and pointed.

A small wagon drawn by two horses emerged from the trees. The box on the back of the rig seemed to be about six foot square. And nearly the same height. One man drove and three stood high in the box. Two more walked behind the rig carrying tools of some kind. After about ten yards the wagon stopped. Shovels appeared in the hands of those in the box. They began tossing loads of something out the back. Gravel, it became clear, as the followers worked the material into the ruts.

With a cold heart, Wade Morgan suddenly knew just where all the explosives in the region ended up. But why? Morgan held his tongue on the theory. This was one time he hoped to be dead wrong.

Not much later the gravel wagon returned following an expensive two place rig drawn by a single horse. The two watchers could not see the driver's face, but he wore an expensive western businessman's outfit. Soon after the two rigs reached the work camp Blue Hawk pointed aloft. The timber structure slowly appeared over the lip of Devil's Tower.

At this range Morgan's binoculars brought him close enough to see various rope rigs attached to the framework. Now a man scrambled out on the structure. He untied several things and let them swing down below the frame. Tied off on a rope he then worked among the hanging parts. Moments later a sturdy small platform hung there. Now two other men appeared. They began to pay out rope to the first man who let it fall straight down. That rope ended at the bottom of a man sized bucket. All three men made sure the heavier line above the bucket sat properly in the twin sheaves of a multiple pulley system. Then the bucket began its descent to trees below.

As the thing neared tree top level Morgan breathed to Blue Hawk, "There's a powerful lot of rope up there. That block and tackle's got a four to one mechanical advantage."

Soon thereafter the bucket rose again. This time it held a passenger. The rope on the bottom of the bucket served to steady the contraption and prevent it from swinging into the Tower's side. Now Morgan and Blue Hawk got a look at the mystery man's face through the binoculars.

During the man's ascent another wagon passed in front of the two watchers. Drawn not by horses, but by six sturdy oxen, the heavy Conestoga seemed to crawl by.

"Explosives, Señor?" whispered the Yaqui.

"That's my guess, Hawk."

As soon as the newcomer exited to the top of the Tower, the crew at the top transfered the bucket to an even more complex block and tackle arrangement and lowered away. Morgan decided that the bucket served simply as ballast to keep the ropes in place. Then the ropes again pulled the rig upward. This time a much larger and heavily padded car appeared over the tops of the trees. A guide rope extended from each of the four corners.

Neither Morgan nor Blue Hawk harbored any doubts as to what now ascended Devils Tower. During the hour long journey the two took turns studying the Tower's face through the binoculars.

At long last Morgan breathed, "Got it, Hawk! There's where they scaled the Tower. See, off to the left. 'Bout twenty yards past that reddish stain. They drove wood stakes into the cracks between the sections. Can barely see them 'cause they're painted black. I figured they wouldn't build directly above their only path down."

The padded rig made three trips to the top during the afternoon. On the third descent the apparent boss rode down in it. The small bucket went back up. As the platform rolled back out of sight the boss' buggy departed, followed in short order by three buckboards filled with tired looking men.

As dusk came two shadows left the observation point in the direction of the Tower. Blue Hawk's usual somber clothing made him difficult to see as they cautiously made their way through the trees. The Yaqui barely saw his companion. For Wade Morgan no longer accompanied his partner. Instead the Masked Rider drifted among the trees like a shadow.

Now the flickering glow of a campfire gave a bit of light to the woods. Very carefully the two Hands of Justice took stock. Five rough looking men sat or stood around the fire. One of them stirred a pot hung over the flames. Another used a bandana over his hand to pull a battered coffee pot off of a small metal grill.

As the two eased closer words came to their ears. Night guards. Shifts were discussed. Then jokes about sleeping in the padded explosives carrier. A sixth man joined them from the direction of the Tower.

"Now, or later, Señor?" hissed Blue Hawk.

The Masked Rider weighed the options for a few seconds, a luxury the two rarely had. Then he whispered, "Now, Hawk. Here's what we'll do."

Ten minutes later Blue Hawk drove the gravel wagon away from Devils Tower. He left the wagon and the six hog-tied men in a ravine more than two miles north.

The Masked Rider wished for a full moon as he grasped the first of the two inch hardwood pegs driven into the side of Devils Tower. His cloak rode in his backpack with gear he hoped he would not need. Coils of rope were tied to his belt. Stout pieces of twine held his six-guns firmly in their holsters. Hawk must think I'm crazy, he decided, as he stepped onto what he believed was the first of at least nine-hundred stakes leading to the top.

Two and a half hours later the Masked Rider inched his aching body over the rim of Devils Tower. Off to the right a small cook fire burned. Two coal oil lanterns gave a lot more light. Here eight men lay and sat in front of three tents. Behind the tents he could see part of the timber platform. He undid the twine on his holsters before he rested.

With the sky fully dark and the night clear, God's Wonder known as the Milky Way arched over Devils Tower. Now rested, the Masked Rider carefully searched the top of the Tower. The slightly domed top of the Tower soon blocked light from the fire. The incredible display in the heavens gave just enough light for the Robin Hood outlaw to safely make his way through the scrub grass and cactus that covered the ground. Occasionally small things moved away as he approached. Once he identified a chipmunk, of all things. He estimated the whole top to be about two-hundred by four-hundred feet.

First he circled the rim looking for more works of man. When the fire came back into sight behind the tents he moved inward. Soon he found a long trench near the center of the area. A large tarpaulin kept out the weather. Into this the Masked Rider slipped. He descended a good ten feet. He walked ahead, his shoulders brushing the sides of the thing. After four steps he found the trench packed tight with wooden cases. Stepping back he risked lighting a match. He could barely make out the other end of the trench over the six foot high run of dynamite cases. He saw no sign of

**The Masked Rider inched
his aching body over the rim...**

blasting caps, or wires. He estimated that one more loaded wagon would be enough to finish filling the trench.

Bud Stone leaned back around the small fire atop Devils Tower. He thought about San Francisco where he intended to spend some of his pay for being marooned in the Blessed sky. Not that the crew that worked for him were bad company. But... One more loading day, then pack the charge. Light the fuze and get the Blue Blazes outta the whole blamed region. And not a day too soon...

A day too late, as it turned out. For out into the firelight stepped a big man dressed all in black. His face covered by a hood, the man's black cloak made him seem even bigger. He held a six-gun confidently in his right hand.

"Nobody move!" came the voice like a roll of distant thunder. Bud Stone blanched. A road-agent twelve-hundred feet above any road.

Then Mart next to him whispered, "The Masked Rider!"

Bud drew breath to speak when the situation got even worse.

A second after he confronted the men the Masked Rider realized he'd made a serious mistake. He did not recount the crew before he stepped into the firelight. Now he only saw seven figures. Two seconds after that the two-hundred pound mistake landed on his back. He barely began to tense for battle when Able Magruder jumped on him.

A strong hand clamped down on the Masked Rider's right forearm. The Robing Hood outlaw spun hard to his right. His left hand flipped his cloak over the attacker's head. Then he ended his spin as hard as he could.

Able Magruder fought to keep his balance. Disoriented and blinded by the hood he gathered himself to try to break the owl-hoot's arm. Then something hard poked him in the stomach. He heard the unmistakable sound of a six-gun cocking.

"Don't!" growled the Masked Rider as he twisted his left hand gun.

Able didn't. Then he let go and stepped away. He could be dead. Should be dead if the man in black rode the outlaw trail.

Bud Stone spoke up, "No gun play, mister. There's a reason we're not armed. You got any idea what a stray bullet could do up here?"

The Masked Rider laughed grimly, "Blow all of us to our choice of Heaven or Hell, friend. I've been in the trench."

Two hours later the Masked Rider and Bud Stone watched by the light of a dozen lanterns as Stone's crew finished carefully emptying the trench. The experienced railroad tunnel blasters knew what they were doing.

"Mister," asked Bud Stone, "just how in Hades did a hard and savvy man like Barton Link get horn-swaggoled like a choir boy?"

"Too much success'd be my guess," replied the Robin Hood outlaw. "Got to thinking he could do bigger things, or anything. When Chinless Smithers convinced him the Tower created the salted diamonds, Link decided to grab the mother lode by splitting Devils Tower."

"An' horn-swoggled me in the process. Convinced me th' Indians would leave the area when the Tower fell so's he could ranch on a huge scale."

"He picked you carefully, Stone. You didn't know much about the real west. Would've been an all out Indian war if whites destroyed this sacred place. Kickin' a nest of rattlesnakes with your bare feet would safer. A whole lot safer."

"When you reach bottom," said the Masked Rider, "my friend will have horses waiting. Head northeast. Don't come anywhere near this area unless you're sure Barton Link's out of business. Good luck."

"Mister, you'll need luck a bunch more'n we will," replied Bud Stone. "And thanks."

With that the eight began their slow descent by the nine hundred pegs.

Whenever the Masked Rider traveled near a library, any kind of library, Wade Morgan tried to find time to visit. Sometimes he virtually camped at such places. Now, all that reading of magazines and scientific journals would again pay off.

Before they left Stone's men hauled the timber structure the full fifty feet past the Tower's edge. They rigged a bosun's chair to the four-to-one block and tackle system. Now the Masked Rider payed out huge amounts of rope down the face of Devils Tower. He put the longest coil of rope available next to the bosun's chair.

Then he lit the six fuses leading to ten cases of dynamite tied down atop the timber structure. Stone assured him that the fuses would burn rain, shine, or morning dew. One or more of the fuses should set the charge off right about dawn.

Fuses sputtering away, the Masked Rider forced himself not to rush back to the bosun's chair. He looped the large coil over his left shoulder, then tied himself into the chair.

Well he remembered the article in the *Scientific American*. He'd transcribed the whole blamed thing, plus traced all the diagrams. To abseil, meaning "to rope down." Jean Estéril Charlet, a native of the French Alps developed a method of safely descending mountainsides and cliffs using controlled friction on the ropes involved. Morgan and Blue Hawk fashioned the "abseil rack," a friction device detailed in the article. After testing, two of the small devices went into the Masked Rider's bag of tricks.

Now the Robin Hood outlaw used the rack to control the speed of the rope feeding through the block and tackle system. More slowly than he wanted he began to descend from the top of Devils Tower.

About two hundred feet above the treetops the flowing rope jammed on something. Descent ceased. Using an evil word or two, the Masked Rider transfered the abseil rack to the end of the large coil of rope. He tied off the end to the bosun's chair and let the coil pay out below. He tied a bowline knot above the rack and stepped into it. Pulling heavy fence making gloves over his cotton ones, he looped a leg around the jammed rope he began to descend via the rack on the free coil.

That coil of rope ran out about fifty feet above the ground. Cursing lividly in three Indian tongues he wrapped the fixed rope around his boot twice and let himself slide. His gloves became hot. His boot began to smell like a freshly branded calf. Then he slid gently into the tree branch snagging the rest of the rope. He shed both sets of gloves. Then he gave a peculiar whistle.

Blue Hawk appeared at the base of the tree a moment later. The Masked Rider bet himself a dollar the Yaqui smiled in the darkness at his predicament.

"Get ready to ride, Hawk. We gotta make Carter's Rock afore dawn!"

Miss Phoenix drew the short straw again at the Queen of the Black Hills. Now she served a pre-dawn breakfast to a big bunch of ill tempered gunmen while their bosses waited impatiently for Barton Link to show for the meeting he called. There wasn't much light in the Queen 'cause she knew Link wanted few townies to know.

What's with this town and dawn? thought Miss Phoenix. The Preacher disappears into the brush and Link aims that telescope in the direction of

Devils Tower. But why? She poured a cup of hot coffee over a groping hand. "Behave, or git it yourself," she told the tables.

About the same time the Masked Rider and Blue Hawk clambered up the the second floor of the Queen. They began checking the rooms.

Barton Link put his eye to the Swiss made telescope mounted in his quarters above his office. Any moment the first rays of the sun would light the Tower long before any of the surrounding area.

Sheriff Chambers roused from his sleep. At first not sure why, he soon realized the noise of hitched up horses on the street seemed far too loud. He slipped on his outfit, checked his gun, and stepped onto the street. Just about then the sky lit up from the direction of Devils Tower.

Ellis Throneberry spun to face the light, and the other flashes that followed. For the shock wave from the ten cases of dynamite on the wood frame blew the cases along the Tower's rim far into the air. Or tried to. A few exploded where they sat. Some more split the air while in flight. The remainder detonated as they impacted the ground and trees. Throneberry raced for town. As he reached the back of his church, the rolling thunderclaps arrived.

Barton Link felt his heart sink when the flash from the tower nearly blinded his one eye. He applied his other eye to the lens in time to see the ring of detonations around the Tower's base. Then rage consumed him. Grabbing his gun belt he sprinted for his saloon to confront the men hired to prevent something like this.

Throneberry reached the street just in time to see Link's maddened face as he dashed into the Queen. The man almost knocked down Miss Phoenix as he crashed through the doors. Unsure of what went on, the man of God snatched up the round pole from the hitching post in front of the Temple of God. Like Moses with a staff he trotted for the saloon.

Sheriff Chambers felt the thunder wash over him. He knew of Barton Link's obsession with Devils Tower. So did half the town. He headed for Link's saloon. Now people streamed out of the nearby buildings, and between them. Some to ask the lawman about the blast. Some to see if Link was responsible. They converged, dressed, and in nightshirts, on the Queen of the Black Hills as their Sheriff pushed through the full closed doors.

Link's furious voice came through the opening. "I've been paying you galoots more'n you're worth to stop things like this! I outta..."

The Masked Rider hoped a fight would break out between Link's men and the hired gangs. In fact, he was about to start it when the Sheriff slammed his way in.

"Hold it right there, Link. You behind this? Hellfire, man! We could have a Indian war outta this."

Link turned. But what he would have said disappeared when a wanted gang leader drew and shot the lawman.

Red Chambers managed half a sidestep before he staggered, a bullet lodged in his gun shoulder. He somehow managed to get the hog-leg out of leather before he had to let go. He fell to the floor as Merry Hades erupted around him.

Too late to stop the first shot, the Masked Rider sent the fast shooting owlhoot leader to Hell with a .45 between the eyes before he could fire again. As his friend's six-gun boomed Blue Hawk slashed the rope holding a huge unlit chandelier above the crowd eating breakfast.

Near a hundred pounds of wood, glass, and metal, crashed directly on several outlaws. Before the unharmed ones could get to their feet the Yaqui began unloading his Winchester into the group.

The Masked Rider leaped over the stair rail to land on the saloon floor with a Colt in each hand. He kept himself between the the gang leaders and the wounded Sheriff. As guns appeared in outlaw hands he fired. And fired.

Barton Link dove for the floor. He wanted no part of the Masked Rider. He scrambled for the main doors.

Miss Phoenix dove for cover. Blood and brains of one owlhoot now stained much of her dress. She headed for the doors only to trip over Barton Link.

The Masked Rider exchanged fire with the outlaw gang leaders. He felt his cloak jerk more than once as bullets pierced the cloth. As the gang leaders fell he fired into the group on the other side of the saloon.

Barton Link shook off confusion from the impact with Miss Phoenix. Suddenly he realized he had a shield to get out of the gunplay. Rearing to his feet he dragged the girl to cover his front. He never noticed the door behind him open. Then he noticed nothing as a heavy staff smashed into his head before he even drew his gun.

Ellis Throneberry gathered up the trembling Miss Phoenix and stuffed her out the door. Then staff in hand he waded into the remaining gang members.

From his position on the stairs Blue Hawk tried to get a bead on Barton Link, but he jerked the girl around too much. Then the wild eyed Padre dashed inside. The pole in his hands snapped Links head forward. Link sprawled as Throneberry steadied the girl, then ran her to safety. The Yaqui respected this bravery. What came next seemed total madness.

The Padre swung the wooden pole left, then right, back, then forward. Almost every swing hit a man. Hard. The malo hombres turned towards him with guns and knives. The pole sent some of the weapons flying. Blue Hawk smiled then. All this madman needed was covering fire. His Winchester spoke now only to protect.

The Masked Rider's right hand gun clicked on a spent chamber. One more round into the overturned tables hiding the rest of the outlaws and his left gun clicked. Heads and guns came quickly into view at the sound. The Robin Hood outlaw dived and rolled across the saloon floor. He scooped up the Sheriff's vintage weapon.

Two more owlhoots met their maker before the sixth round left the Confederate gun. When the firing stopped the remaining heads popped up again. One fool stood and stepped toward the man in black while he added cartridges to his six-gun.

Blam! Blam! Blam! The gun bucked three times in the Masked Rider's hand. The heads at the table disappeared. Forever.

The astonished gun loader swore. "You gotta be out, now!" he exclaimed with a smile as he rammed in the last round.

While the fool spoke the Masked Rider pivoted the Cavalry pistol's hammer forward. Then he pulled the trigger. The charge of shot in the center of the weapon's cylinder literally wiped the smile off the outlaw's face.

In the silence that followed the Masked Rider looked over to see Ellis Throneberry standing amid a tall pile of battered bodies. There was not a mark on him.

"Thunderation, Parson!" exclaimed the masked man. "How'd you manage that?"

Throneberry felt the rage drain from him. He looked back across the saloon. "I hear some call you the Robin Hood outlaw, friend. When I was a lad, a Welshman taught me, and his own son, how to use Robin Hood's quarterstaff."

A very rare sound reached the Masked Rider then. The sound of Blue Hawk's laugh of welcome surprise.

Shortly the Masked Rider thundered out of town. In an arroyo beyond the Preacher's benches the Robin Hood Outlaw disappeared. Not long after Wade Morgan galloped into Carter's Rock on the pinto. He fained astonishment at the carnage inside the Queen of the Black Hills saloon. The barber still tended to the surviving wounded. So had Blue Hawk, to judge by the blood spattered and smeared on his clothing. The Yaqui calmly stacked the dead in one corner of the saloon. Miss Phoenix directed the rest of the girls in caring for a few townies injured by flying lead or glass. The Parson recited prayers as he stood next to the dead. Morgan went right to where the wounded Sheriff lay.

"That hombre in black was right. Stopped me on the trail. Told me the town needed help. What can I do?"

"Glad you came, Morgan," grunted the Sheriff as he tried to find a less painful position. "The town folk're good people, bless 'em. But, ain't a lawman among 'em. That Indian already locked up them that needed it for me. An' Miss Phoenix has the grit. But the blessed law says I can only make white men inta deputies..."

In almost the time it takes to tell Wade Morgan, himself a highly wanted man, got a star pinned to his chest. With with the help of the Sheriff, the Preacher, and Miss Phoenix, he finished sorting out the Link's men. Both the dead and the living. Then he began taking statements. About that time Blue Hawk vanished. Morgan ended up mighty glad the lawyer and a former school marm did most of the writing.

The aftermath of the Masked Rider's wrath was something Wade Morgan rarely saw. This time he knew he couldn't just ride into the sunrise. By the time statements were done, the sin rooms of the saloon changed into hospital rooms. And the scarlet ladies into temporary nurses. Most of the patients were shackled to the beds.

The wives of the town brought food for those working. About an hour after dinner time Ellis Throneberry asked if he was still needed. Morgan glanced at the now sleeping Sheriff, thanked the man of God, and bid him good evening. Ten minutes later he saw Miss Phoenix slip out a side door headed in the direction of the Temple of God.

Ellis Throneberry stood at the Alter to God he built with his own hands. For the tenth time he scanned through his Bible's thick Concordance seeking the proper verse to ease his soul from the violence he had done that day. His inner mind kept repeating, "The more I hurt, the fewer died."

In the town's prevailing silence he heard the church door open, then be quietly closed. He stood still as hesitant steps came most of the way down the center aisle.

He turned, expecting to greet a member of his congregation. Instead, in her fine and bloodstained dress, there stood Miss Phoenix. She stood stock still as he faced her. Then she drew in a breath.

"Preacher, I want forgiveness." Her lips quivered as she spoke. "I'm begging for forgiveness."

Ellis smiled. "The Lord forgives all who believe and sincerely repent of their sins."

"I know that Preacher. I know He forgives me. But I also want *your* forgiveness. For that day. Link knew I'd been atalkin' to you. Then one day he told me you'd paid him for me to call on you. Professionally. That you wanted to sin with me here in the church. But that I had to ask for the meeting so it'd look like I was trying to be saved. And dadgumit, I believed him. And you, about the only one in town didn't treat me like trash. Please Preacher... Please, forgive me."

She broke contact with his eyes as she began to sob. Slowly she sank to her knees in the middle of the aisle. Throneberry turned to place the Bible back on the alter. Then he walked to her huddled form. Kneeling in front of her, he placed a hand on each of her shoulders.

" Miss Phoenix... Phoenix, you were tricked." Then he told her firmly, "There is *nothing* to forgive."

She sobbed even harder then, but the sobs were those of relief, and then, perhaps, joy. Gingerly, he pulled her to him. She clung to him as he let his hands fall to his sides. "Phoenix," he whispered, "now, like the mythical bird, you can rise from the ashes of your old life."

"Dora, Preacher. Please call me Dora."

"Only if you call me Ellis. Now, come on. I'll put on a pot of coffee. I think we have a lot to talk about."

From a shadowed corner of the sanctuary Wade Morgan quietly slipped out the side door. He headed to the town jail, of all places, with a satisfied smile on his face.

THE END

How I met the Masked Rider, and Other Western Avengers

Like most Americans my age, I grew up on westerns. There were western (and Northern) radio shows like James Stewart in "The Sixshooter," and the modern day Sky King. Sgt. Preston ("The Challenge of the Yukon") and the "Silver Eagle" kept the peace in the wilder parts of Canada. And, most importantly for the younger set, "The Lone Ranger" hit the trail three times a week.

Most of the movies I got taken to in suburban St. Louis were either swashbucklers or westerns. These were the "A" movies. I never saw "B" westerns until we got a TV set. In my crowd Hopalong Cassidy ruled the TV roost. We didn't like singing cowboys, or too much comedy relief. Sorry, Roy and Gene. We pretty much ignored you. We also got to meet folks like Johnnie Mack Brown and Lash LaRue on TV, but the only masked man we knew was that fellow named Reid.

And comics were much the same. At least Roy and Gene didn't sing there. And the sidekicks were more subdued. But only the Lone Ranger had a mask, or a secret identity. (DC and Atlas/Marvel westerns got almost no distribution in our area.)

One summer, about 1962 or '63, I explored every used book store I could find in Albuquerque, New Mexico. In the back of one I found a stack of coverless comic books. All the same issue of something called *Best Of The West*. I'd never heard of Red Mask (actor Tim Holt as Red Mask, but only in the comics), or The Darango Kid. Those films never played St. Louis TV. I knew Straight Arrow only from the activity cards given away as layer dividers in Nabisco Shredded Wheat. But I had definitely heard of the Ghost Rider. I later learned Straight Arrow also had a secret identity. He was a white man who masqueraded as a Comanche warrior while catching bad guys of both races. (I'll have to fit him into a Jim Anthony story some day.)

Then I noticed a pulp magazine lying nearby. I'd see any number of late western and detective and pulps in my shopping. I knew a bit about the Shadow pulps after the recent radio revival. But this cover stood out. Here was a cowboy with a domino mask, and a black hat. He also wore a black cape lined with red. Wait a second! This was the hero? Had to be. The magazine's title was *Masked Rider Western* from 1952. So I bought it.

"Deadline For Sheep" was the name of the Masked Rider story. Decades later I discovered that the lead novel carried the same story format restrictions as all Thrilling hero pulps after the end of World War Two. The bad guy was allowed only two, or at the most three, henchmen, plus maybe a second in command because the boss's identity was a mystery with no more than four suspects. This formula applied to the Phantom Detective and the Black Bat, as well as the Masked Rider. Still this left room to spin an exciting adventure. I liked the novel and even picked up one or two other late issues of the title at conventions.

Then, in 1970, I found two paperback reprints of Masked Rider stories from about 1938. What a difference! This Masked Rider faced down hordes of badmen. Body counts seemed as high as the new Mack Bolan/ Executioner stories I began reading at about the same time. A couple of decades after that I picked up an even earlier pulp issue. Seems another company started the character. They folded after a dozen issues. Then Thrilling picked it up.

The earliest Masked Rider wore all black, including cloak and a full face mask. And Blue Hawk wore Mexican style clothing. Sure, things seemed an awful lot like the Lone Ranger. But there were important differences. One was that the never named Masked Rider often appeared as Wade Morgan, a cowboy drifter. Plus Blue Hawk, thanks to attending Mission schools, spoke and read proper Spanish and English.

My stories of the Masked Rider and Blue Hawk include all of these original differences.

To see Blue Hawk on his own check out my story in the Pulp Spirit online magazine at:

http://www.planetarystories.com/bluehawk.htm

ERWIN K. ROBERTS - grew up watching western movies and television. He read some western comics and even a few of the Lone Ranger novels. But he still remembers western radio drama, as well.

He's lived in the far west, sort of. The Presidio of San Francisco to be exact. But he did spend a short time on maneuvers with the Army in the desert areas of New Mexico. Which was definitely better that the mosquito infested swamps of Key Largo he had to return to.

Starting about 1980 Erwin began appearing on the Public Access cable channel in Kansas City, Missouri. He reviewed movies, books, and the occasional comic. He interviewed actors, writers, artists, gaffers & grips, and a Klingon, or two.

But before that Erwin is particularly proud that his first ever celebrity interview was with Clayton Moore. Moore visited Kansas City about three weeks after he was forced to wear those big sunglasses, instead of the Lone Ranger's mask. He told the press that he would get the mask back. Took a while, but by gosh he did it.

These days Erwin is exploring the opportunities offered by retirement. He and his wife plan to travel quite a bit now that they have both given up the rat race. (What's so fun about racing rats, anyway?) In the meantime he continues to pound the keyboard. Sometimes this activity even produces understandable English.

Erwin can be reached at erwin.k.roberts@gmail.com

THE MASKED RIDER

"The Vultures of Yellow Mesa"

by Bill Craig

Wade Morgan swung out of the saddle dropping down to wrap Cutter's reins around the hitching post. The Lazy Dog saloon was doing what appeared to be a booming business. Laughter and piano music were audible through the batwings. Without appearing to, Morgan slipped the hammer thongs off of his guns. Sometimes it was better to be prepared for trouble than not. Most times in fact. From what he and Blue Hawk had been hearing, this little town in the shadow of Yellow Mesa was in a bind and he meant to do something about it. If it turned out to be too much for Wade Morgan, then The Masked Rider would step in.

It bothered him that Clanton's Folly seemed more like a ghost town than a thriving western town which was what it had a reputation for. The mine at Yellow Mesa had been a profitable one for several years now, unlike its predecessor for which the town had been named. For a boom town, it was too quiet. And there were not many new people coming in, even with word going out of a big strike. Morgan wanted to know why.

His spurs jingled as Morgan stepped up on the boardwalk, taking a quick glance around. A fly buzzed slowly past him in the still afternoon air. He pushed through the batwings and immediately stepped to the side of the door, giving his eyes a chance to adjust to the dimmer light inside while not making a target standing in the door.

Morgan had been on the trail for many days and he looked it, with a weeks worth of stubble and dust-covered clothing. He looked very much the part he was playing, that of a drifting cowhand riding the grubline and looking for work. Blue Hawk was a couple of days behind him. He would be bringing Midnight along with him.

Morgan had felt it would be less noticeable if he just showed up with Cutter. The gray roan was a fairly common sight on the plains and prairie. The music never wavered and few of the patrons if any paid much attention to him. Morgan made his way to the bar and ordered up a beer. The bartender filled a mug and set it in front of him and Morgan handed him two bits. The bartender frowned at the coins and made his way on down the bar. Morgan hid a smile as he took a sip of beer and scanned the room with his icy blue eyes.

The beer tasted good as it cut the trail dust from his throat. The glint of sunlight off a tin star caught his eye. The Sheriff sat in a corner, a bottle of whiskey open on the table beside him. Morgan noted that the bottle was half-empty, and the shot glass in front of the Sheriff had just recently been filled. Morgan moseyed over to the table and dropped into a seat across from the sheriff. He could see the man across from him as well as keep an eye on the bat-winged front doors.

"Howdy, Sheriff. You know where a man might find a job here abouts?" Morgan smiled.

"Around here? A man would be a damned fool to come around here," The Sheriff shook his head.

"Wade Morgan, Sheriff. I've been called damned fool before and I wore the name well," Morgan took another sip of his beer. The Sheriff lifted his head and looked at him through bleary eyes.

"Didn't you hear me the first time, kid?" he asked.

"I did, but I'm about out of money and I need work. Food don't often come free," Morgan shrugged, taking another sip of beer.

"Ain't no work to be had around here," the Sheriff shook his head. He tossed back the shot of whiskey and made a face as it burned its way down his throat.

"What about the mine?" Morgan probed.

"Closed for the duration," the Sheriff replied, shaking his head.

"The duration of what?" Morgan asked.

"Feller, mind your own business. Ride on out and don't look back," the Sheriff glared at him.

"Something is wrong here, Sheriff. What is it?" Morgan took a long pull at his beer.

"Get out of here, drifter, before I throw your sorry butt in jail," the Sheriff growled, his eyes small and mean.

"No need to get testy, Sheriff. After I finish my drink I'll move on," Wade shook his head. Something was definitely wrong in Clanton's Folly. Why would the mine close when it was producing so well? Why was the Sheriff turning into a drunk? Those were questions that needed to be answered. Morgan knew that there was no way that he would leave before he had the answers. Knowing that he would get no more from the sheriff, Morgan stood and walked back to the bar.

Morgan surveyed the room, looking to see if there was anyone else he might gain information from. He looked at the bartender. The man was a few feet away with slicked down black hair and a large handlebar mustache. "Bartender," Morgan called. With a look of disdain, the bartender moved down the bar to where he was standing.

"What do you want?" the bartender glared at him with a look of near hatred in his eyes.

"Another beer would be nice. Any ranches hiring here abouts?" Morgan asked, draining his mug.

"Not that I know of. Strangers ain't welcome around here. Too much trouble when strangers ride in," the bartender shook his head, sat a fresh mug of beer in front of him and moved back down the bar as if he were expecting trouble. Morgan pushed his gray Stetson back on his head. Clanton's Folly beat anyplace he'd ever seen. It was right unfriendly.

One thing that also caught his attention was that none of the girls working the saloon came near him. Now while he certainly wasn't a beauty, Morgan knew from experience that women found him attractive, and yet none of the gals in the saloon gave him a second look.

Morgan sipped his beer. Despite the apparent gaiety in the saloon there was an undercurrent of fear that ran deep. Fear and desperation. They were trying hard to make everything appear normal, and by doing so had showed that something was wrong. Morgan did nothing to let his inner thoughts show on his face, maintaining the friendly affable masquerade that Wade Morgan was. Sensing that nothing more would be accomplished in the saloon, Morgan downed his beer and headed for the door.

About that time the batwings swung open and two mean wearing long white dusters stepped inside. Morgan smiled to himself. Somebody had spread the word that a stranger was in town. Morgan continued towards the door, moving in an easy unthreatening gait towards the newcomers. He was aware that the saloon had gone so silent as to hear a pin drop.

"What do you want around here?" the first man glared at him.

"Who's askin'?" Morgan asked in his slow easy manner. Under the surface his muscles were coiled like tightly wound springs, ready to strike and snatch his guns at the first provocation.

"I am," the man replied coldly.

"You got a name?" Morgan asked, still grinning.

"Stockton," the man replied.

"Good, I hate killing a man when I don't know his name," Morgan nodded.

"What?" Stockton looked surprised as did the man with him. Before they could react Morgan's guns were in his hands and blazing away. The two duster-clad men stumbled backwards, bloody flowers blossoming on their chests. Their guns never even cleared leather. They hit the floor at the same time, their boots drumming a final tattoo on the floorboards.

Morgan stepped away from the tables and spun to face the room, his six-shooters still in his hands and ready to roar if needed. An older man at one of the tables looked at him.

"You looking for a job son?" the man asked.

"I am," Morgan replied. He noticed that the sheriff sat unmoving in the corner, still sucking down whiskey like there was no tomorrow.

"I'm Sam Tillman. I own the Double D ranch outside of town. I could use a fighter like you," the man said.

"I don't sell my guns, Tillman. But if I hire on, I ride for the brand. If that leads to lead throwing, then I'm as game as anybody. I just want that understood," Morgan looked at the man.

"Fifty a month and found. Fighting wages. Considering what we have for law in this town, we need some good men," Tillman nodded.

"You want to lead the way?" Morgan smiled as he slipped the empty cartridges from his Smith & Wesson Russian .44s and loaded fresh loads into them.

"That's a reasonable enough request," Tillman chuckled.

"You're asking for trouble, Tillman," the Sheriff called from his table.

"At least I'm doing something, Norton," Tillman shook his head in disgust.

"The Sheriff always so friendly?" Morgan asked as he followed Tillman out of the Lazy Dog Saloon.

"Here lately," Tillman shook his head.

"What about them two boys that came in looking for trouble?" Morgan probed gently, searching for information.

"No good varmints. They ride for Duke Wilson. There's been nothing but trouble since he moved into the area. They been rustling my cattle as well. Nobody around here seems to have the guts to go up against them. I got to tell you in advance, son, we're bucking a stacked deck," Tillman told him.

"Well, I never figured to get rich punching cows," Morgan shrugged as he unhitched Cutter's reins and swung into the saddle atop the gray horse.

"Riding for me may well get you dead," Tillman shook his head, climbing into the saddle of his own horse.

"There's been a few Jaspers that tried to accomplish that, but so far ain't none of them had much luck," Morgan grinned. If only Tillman knew how many men had tried to kill him since he had taken up the mantle of the Masked Rider.

"Well don't get too cocky, fella. Them are some right salty old boys riding for Wilson. He managed to buffalo the whole town. I ain't worked out exactly how yet, but I'm working on it," Tillman told him. Morgan nodded.

It was something that he wanted to know as well. It took a lot to tree a western town. So Wilson had to have something big to run roughshod over the townspeople the way that he was. It was a mystery for the Masked Rider for sure!

Sheriff Cole Norton watched the two men ride out of town. He had stopped on his way out of the saloon to spit on the bodies of Stockton and Grange. He hoped that Wilson would not take it out on Lucy Moore and Claudia Chapman. Poor Lucy. Norton shook his head, feeling the tears welling up in his eyes. If she had only stayed in the store that day instead of trying to run across the street to stop him. Then Wilson would never have seen her, never have gained a hold over him. But the outlaw chief had.

Norton felt nausea washing up within him and staggered into an alley to vomit. Let the town think he had lost his nerve. Until Lucy was safe, there was nothing he could do against Duke Wilson. And poor Frank Chapman, the rancher never had a chance after Wilson's men took Claudia. The rancher dotted on her and would do anything to protect her. The thought of either of the women in the hands of Duke Wilson was almost too much for him to bear.

Wilson had a reputation for being especially brutal, and his treatment of women had the reward for his capture up in the hundred of thousands of dollars range. He was an animal of the worst kind, and a killer that killed without distinction or remorse. Norton headed for his office. He had a couple of fresh bottles of whiskey at the jail. If he was lucky, he would pass out soon.

Lucy Moore wiped her hands on her apron. Cooking for her captors wasn't a whole lot different than cooking for her father and Cole. The only difference was that right now, she was being forced to do it. She wasn't sure exactly where she was, someplace in the mountains outside town. She had been able to ascertain that from the window. She had been blindfolded when she had been brought here. So, from what she had been able to ascertain in the few private moments she had gotten to speak with her had Claudia Chapman.

Duke Wilson had kept the two women apart as much as possible since they had arrived. Lucy was fairly sure that it was to keep them from putting their heads together and plotting to escape. As long as he held them prisoner, both the Sheriff and Claudia's father wouldn't dare move against them. Lucy sighed, brushing a stray lock of blonde hair away from her face.

At times it seemed hopeless, and then others, she had and was able to hold onto the faintest glimmer of hope. She prayed the Cole Norton would come riding in with a posse to rescue her. But with each passing day, that hope grew a little dimmer.

Cole was a good man, but he was no hero. Lucy was beginning to understand that more with each passing day. It would take a man with a lot of sand to stand up to Duke Wilson. The bandit leader was a known killer and robber and rapist. Lucy felt relieved that he had made no advanced towards her, nor had he allowed any of his men to do so. It seemed to be his one redeeming quality so far.

"Woman, bring some more of that stew," roared one of the outlaw band. Choking back a sob, Lucy ladled more stew into a pot and turned to carry it back into the other room. She took a deep breath and let it out slowly. She would not let them see her cry! Lucy carried the pot back out into the main room and set it on the table.

Duke Wilson sat at the far end of the table, watching her. Lucy flinched slightly, but tried not to show it. So far, Wilson had done nothing out of the way, she hoped that would continue. She ladled more stew into the bowls in front of his men.

"Go to your room. You can clean this up later," Wilson growled at her. Lucy nodded and fled the room, going to the bedroom that she and Claudia Chapman shared. Claudia was in the barn doing other chores for the moment. Lucy wondered why Wilson had ordered her to her room. He must, she figured, be planning something with his men that he didn't want her to know. The thought frightened her.

Blue Hawk led the horses into a small valley. It looked like a good place to set up camp. There was plenty of graze for the horses and plenty of water. He had shot a mule deer the day before and dressed it out. He had set up a place to smoke the meat in a small stand of trees that would deflect the smoke and make it far less noticeable. The half-breed warrior had learned long ago the best places and ways to establish a camp where it didn't look like one.

Half-Mexican and half Yaqui, Blue Hawk knew the desert like the back of his hand. He was just as good in the mountains. Morgan had asked him to meet him here in the shadow of Yellow Mesa. He had never questioned the other man's orders once Morgan had saved his life. Never mind that he had saved Morgan's life first. As far as Blue Hawk was concerned, he owed Morgan and his alter ego of the Masked Rider a debt that he could never repay.

Blue Hawk ground reined the Black Stallion Midnight and Moonwind while he had set up his camp. Now he saw to the horses, removing the bridles and saddles and letting them run for a bit. Neither of them would stray far. Blue Hawk wondered how long it would be before he heard from Wade Morgan. He was sure it would not take long. He could sense the tension in the air; Yellow Mesa was a troubled place. Tomorrow he would take Moonwind and ride into town to look the situation over. Blue Hawk fixed a small supper and then rolled into his blankets after putting out the cook fire. The next day would be a long one.

Wade Morgan kept an eye all around as the sun sank down in the west. He didn't know Tillman well enough to trust him, but he instinctively liked the man and his instincts had never let him down before.

"Sam, just what in tarnation is going on around these parts. I heard that the area around Yellow Mesa and Clanton's Folly was right friendly and prosperous. That a fella could get work easy enough if he wanted it and was willing to put in a good days work for a good days pay," Wade looked at his new employer.

"Young fella, every since Duke Wilson and his men moved into the territory that has all changed. People are walking more nervous and tense. Trouble when it comes, comes with bullets flying and they ain't too particular where or who they hit," Tillman replied. Morgan thought about that for a while.

"Seems like Wilson and his gang are throwing a mighty wide loop," Morgan tilted his hat back.

"They do. I'm still trying to figure out exactly why," Tillman nodded.

"When did folks start acting nervous?" Morgan looked over at Tillman.

"Well I knew they were in the territory before I went into town. In the week or so since I had been to town it had all changed," Tillman shrugged.

"Strikes me as funny how quick them fellers showed up after I got to the saloon," Morgan noted.

"Sure does. Almost like they had somebody lookin' out for strangers. You ride easy boy when you are out on the range. Don't go taking no fool chances on my account," Tillman shook his head.

"I ride for the brand, Boss. I'll do what I believe will best serve the interests of the Double D," Morgan replied, meaning it. He had a feeling that the Double D was somehow a threat to whatever Duke Wilson was planning on doing in these parts.

"I believe you boy. But I don't want you to go gettin' yourself killed for no good reason," Tillman sighed.

"I for sure don't plan on it boss," Morgan chuckled.

"Duke Wilson and his boys are pure poison. So far, they ain't bothered the Double D much. Except for some minor rustling. I figure that's likely to change," Tillman explained.

"I figure you're right. How many boys you got on the Double D?" Morgan was curious. Good fighting men could make all the difference in the world if it came down to shooting.

"Counting you? About fifteen salty old boys," Tillman grinned.

"That ought a be plenty," Morgan nodded.

"We turn off here," Tillman nodded at a big rock near the road.

"That fella with the rifle gonna have problems with that? Morgan asked, slipping the hammer thongs off his guns.

"Hank, this fella spotted you. You might want to work on that," Tillman called.

"I will Boss. I rose up when I heard two sets of hooves for a better look," Hank shook his head.

"Might try taking your hat off when watching then. It gave you away," Morgan called out.

"I'll remember that," Hank stood up.

"Hank, this is Wade Morgan. I hired him in town after he put down two of Wilson's boys," Tillman said by way of introduction. Morgan heard Hank whistle.

"I'd sure like to have seen that," Hank nodded.

"I'm taking him on to the bunkhouse to meet the boys. Figured you ought to know who he was so you wouldn't be taking pot shots at him like you did Clay," Tillman said.

"Aw now that was an accident. I didn't expect Clay to come riding in from the opposite direction of town," Hank shook his head.

"No reason you should, except it was broad daylight," Tillman stuck the needle to his hand. Morgan hid a grin, recognizing what was going on for what it was. He realized that Hank knew it too.

"Would you send Shorty to out when you get to the bunkhouse? It's time for him to take over anyways," Hank called after them.

"Sure thing, Hank," Tillman called over his shoulder. Morgan chuckled as they rode down the dusty lane towards the ranch house and the outbuildings.

"Boss, it sure sounds like you got an interesting bunch working for you," Morgan shook his head.

"They are at that," Tillman nodded.

Duke Wilson was sitting on the front porch of the log cabin drinking coffee when one of his men came fogging up in a cloud of dust. It was obvious that he had ridden the horse hard, almost as if he had the hounds of hell on his heels. It was Fletcher, one of the men he had left in town to keep an eye on things. Fletcher stumbled after sliding out of the saddle and almost fell on his face he was in such an all fired hurry.

"Boss!" he shouted.

"Why the hell are you here instead of in town like you're supposed to be?" Duke's voice was quiet and still as the grave. Duke stood up, having slipped the hammer thong off his gun as he did so.

"I got news, Boss! Some stranger rode into town today and kilt two of the boys in the saloon!" Fletcher gasped for breath.

"Any idea who he was?" Wilson eyed the man before him. Fletcher was a slacker and a coward unless he had the whole band behind him.

"Nope, but Sam Tillman hired him to work for him right on the spot," Fletcher said.

"Tillman, eh. Anybody else take a shine to him?" Duke nodded thoughtfully.

"Nope Boss, nobody but Tillman. Sheriff just stood by and let it happen," Fletcher shook his head, taking off his hat to mop the sweat off his face.

"So why didn't he shoot you too, Fletcher?" Duke's voice turned to ice.

"I reckon 'cause I wasn't with them," Fletcher shrugged.

"Why is that Fletcher?" Wilson glared at the outlaw who was starting to shake where he stood.

"I was up at the Silver Dollar with one of the girls, Boss. I heard about it all afterwards and came to tell you as quick as I could," Fletcher swallowed audibly.

"That is the only reason you're still breathing Fletch. I can tell you came first thing. Rub that Bay down and get her fed and watered and then get another mount from the corral and get your lazy ass back to town. Any more strangers ride in, I want to know it before anybody else gets killed," Wilson commanded. Fletcher's head was bobbing up and down in agreement.

Shaking his head, Wilson walked back to his chair. He took another drink of his coffee as he sat down again. Tillman was going to be a problem. He hadn't been able to get anything on the owner of the Double D to keep him in line. That was going to have to change.

"Boss!" he shouted.

Wade Morgan had found himself a spot in the bunkhouse after meeting the rest of Tillman's crew. They seemed to a man to be solid capable cowboys that rode for the brand. He enjoyed the rare camaraderie of the bunkhouse banter that had ended only as each of them drifted off to sleep. Tonight, he would not be able to slip away as much as he wanted to. No, the Masked Rider had to stay away from Yellow Mesa for the moment.

There was certainly plenty to investigate, from the way the town was acting to the Sheriff's decidedly lack-luster efforts at law enforcement in Yellow Mesa. There was also the matter of Duke Wilson and his gang. What had brought them to Yellow Mesa and why were they staying in the area?

A lot of questions for sure. He hoped to be able to answer them pretty soon. Wade Morgan rolled his blankets tight around him and closed his eyes. He had a feeling that he'd be up with the sun and getting started earning some pay as a working cowboy. He smiled to himself. It had been a while since he had done that…

Blue Hawk's eyes opened as he heard the sound of a horse moving close to the camp. The fire had died out earlier and the moon was near the horizon. Blue Hawk found his knife and drew it silently. He slowly snaked out from under the blanket, arranging them to look like he was still under them. The Yaqui could move as silent as a ghost when he wanted to, and right now he wanted to.

Blue Hawk ghosted into the trees and waited, eyes searching the night. He could hear the horse moving, the faint jingle of spurs. Someone was searching for something. Blue Hawk waited. The horse moved off, away from the camp. Blue Hawk stayed where he was for another hour, and when the horizon was starting to lighten, Blue Hawk moved back to his bedroll and covered up once more and went back to sleep.

Cole Norton sat in a chair in front of his office looking out at the night. He had a bottle of whiskey that he took long swallows from. He wiped his lips as the warmth spread through his belly. Norton looked at the bottle and the amber-colored liquor inside it. He hated what it was making him, but what choice did he have? If he had stood up to Wilson he would be buried out on Boot Hill. "Why?" he asked himself. Why had Lucy chosen the moment she had to run out into the street?

She had deliberately put herself at risk as he had faced Wilson. Norton knew he had little chance against a gunman of Wilson's reputation; Lucy had just given him an excuse to not even try. Norton could feel the tears welling in his eyes and streaming down his cheeks. Lucy would stay unharmed as long as he let Wilson and his men run roughshod over the town. What sort of lawman did that make him?

Norton shook his head and reached up to wipe the tears away. He was coward of the worst sort. He had put the woman he loved in mortal danger and had done nothing to stop it. The worst part was that he knew she knew it. She had seen the relief in his eyes that he wouldn't have to face the outlaw's guns. She had given him a look that was worse than her getting angry would have. She had looked at him like he was the most pitiful wretch she had ever seen, and what made it worse was that she was right.

Norton took another long pull at the bottle. Maybe he should just get out of town, ride away into the night and never come back. But if he did that, what would happen to Lucy? Cole Norton knew he wasn't much of a man, but he also knew he just couldn't ride away and leave her to the clutches of Duke Wilson. He had to find some way to rescue her. Norton climbed to his feet, still clutching the near empty bottle and staggered inside the jail, bolting the door behind him. Not to keep anyone in, but to keep everyone else out.

⁂

Duke Wilson had slipped away from his camp and had ridden towards the far side of Yellow Mesa. His partner had wanted to meet far away from the prying eyes of town. Duke had reached the meeting place early, as was his way. Wilson trusted no one, least of all his own men. He trusted his partner even less, but Wilson had to admit that the money was good.

So far, the mines had made no move to ship any of the gold out, but they couldn't wait much longer. The miners wanted their pay, and Wilson knew from his spies in town that they were starting to get inpatient about it. His horse nickered and Wilson was instantly alert. His horse was a better sentry than any man could be. Wilson slipped his Colt from leather and thumbed back the hammer as he saw a dark silhouette ride up. The man stayed back just far enough that Wilson couldn't make out his face in the shadows.

"They're getting ready to ship the gold. If they wait any longer and the miners will tear the place apart," the man in the shadows announced his voice not more than a harsh whisper.

"When?" Wilson grinned.

"The end of the week, no later," his partner replied.

"What about the rest of it?" Wilson asked.

"Don't get greedy, Duke. There's plenty for us both if you'll be patient. The Bank's got a shipment coming in this week as well. Follow my lead and we'll both be rich," the man in the shadows said.

"Well the boys will be happy when we get to do more than run off cows. They want some gold in their pockets and a chance to spend it," Wilson shrugged.

"Meet me here in two nights and I'll have a job for them that they'll like," his unknown partner said, then he turned his horse and rode off into the night. Wilson watched him go, listening to the way his horse ran. He nodded. It had an odd gait. That information could prove useful later on. Wilson waited until the sound of hoofbeats had faded into the night.

Wilson climbed into the saddle and headed back towards the hideout. More and more he was wondering who his mysterious partner was. He would have to do a little nosing around on his own and maybe he would find the answers.

Wade Morgan twisted in his blankets, cold sweat pouring out of his body as he lay in the grip of a nightmare. Images filled his dreams, stark and vivid. He could feel the heat of the flames, hear the screams and the sounds of gunshots, feel the bullets pound into his flesh. He sat up quickly, stifling a cry. The last thing he wanted to do was wake the rest of the cowboys in the bunk house up.

Morgan wiped the sweat off his face with his blanket and lay back down. He doubted if he would actually sleep any more this night. Too many memories were crowding in his head. He heard the door to the bunkhouse open and watched through slitted eyes as someone entered and slipped into bed on the other side of the room. He would have to see who that bunk belonged to in the morning.

A soft moan escaped his lips and there was a noise from the other bunk. Morgan silently cursed the involuntary noise he had made. He watched the other man rise and move towards him. Morgan closed his eyes and moaned again, deliberately this time, purposely thrashing on his bunk and throwing off the covers, sitting up suddenly.

"You okay, fella?" asked a whispered voice.

"Bad dream," Morgan mumbled, laying back down and pulling the cover back over himself.

"Well keep it down. All the noise you're making is making it damn hard to sleep," the other voice whispered.

"Sorry," Morgan mumbled. He smiled to himself, knowing that he had fooled the man, at least for the moment. Still, he would find out the man's identity, and when he did it could lead him to finding out what was going on around Yellow Mesa.

_____ ❧ ❧ _____

The bunkhouse crew rose well before the sun was up and that was fine with Morgan. He hadn't gone back to sleep anyway. When the first lamp had been lit, Morgan had rolled to his feet and pulled on his pants and boots over his long handles. He pulled a shirt out of his saddle bags and put it on. He glanced at the bunk, taking note of the man's face before heading for the outhouse to take care of business and stopping at the rain barrel to wash his face.

The cook had risen even earlier and had biscuits and gravy, bacon and eggs all cooked up and a mess of flap jacks as well with real maple syrup and honey. Wade Morgan felt obligated to eat his share of the breakfast fare. A fella by the name of Clint Rawlings was the Segundo of the Double D and he sized up as a fairly smart man. Morgan respected him instantly as he gave them their marching orders for the day. The orders were good ones and were what Morgan would have done under the circumstances as well.

Morgan was partnered up with a Mexican named Alvarez and a cowboy called Skip for the way that he walked. Both had an easy sense of humor and easy dispositions. Both were also hard workers and in little time after reaching the high country they had a small herd bunched together to move out of the mountains into the lower pasture closer to the ranch house. By Morgan's tally they had nearly 300 head ready to move. That was when the other riders came.

_____ ❧ ❧ _____

Morgan and Alvarez had just pushed another fifty head out of a break when they spotted the six riders approaching the larger heard that Skip had been holding in place. Morgan shucked his Winchester from the boot and spurred his horse ahead to reach Skip, leaving Alvarez to finish with the ones they were bringing out.

"Who are them boys?" Wade Morgan asked as he reached Skip.

"Can't say for sure 'til they get close enough to see their faces, but they don't none of them look familiar," Skip pushed his hat back on his head. He'd already slipped the hammer thong off his Colt and drew his Winchester and had it sitting across his saddle horn ready to use.

"I'm gonna move off a bit and put some distance between us so we ain't all bunched up," Morgan spat.

"Good idea," Skip nodded. He took out his makings and built him a smoke as the riders drew nearer. Wade Morgan had moved off about twenty feet to his left and he heard Alvarez ride up on his right. The riders drew to a halt about ten yards from him. Skip turned his horse slightly so that the muzzle of the Winchester covered the leader of the group.

"Hello, Gents, what can I do for ya?" Skip called across the distance.

"How about you just turn them cows over to us?" the leader of the group smiled.

"How about you just scoop up a cow pie and commence to eating it?" Skip called back, knowing what was coming. He eared back the hammer of the Winchester with an audible click.

"Now that wasn't a friendly comment, son," the man replied, his expression hard.

"Wasn't meant to be and you ain't my pa so don't go calling me son," Skip replied.

"You're right about that. If'n you was my son I'd take that gun away from you and spank you with it," the man said.

"You got it to do. Just keep in mind you'll be the first one blowed out of the saddle," Skip said in a matter of fact tone.

"Hell Boss, there is only three of 'em," one of the other men muttered.

"And we'll clear three saddles before you get a shot off," Wade Morgan added. "We might take some lead, but you won't be around to know it." The implication hung heavy in the air.

"You're a right salty bunch ain't you?" the leader grinned.

"You got it to find out," Wade Morgan grinned.

"I don't think so. Not today anyways," the leader grinned.

"In that case I figure you best clear off of Double D range. 'Cause if we see you again on our range, next time we won't be so polite," Morgan told them.

"Nope, I reckon not. Can't say as I blame you either. We'll be on our way then," the leader said.

"You got a name?" Morgan asked.

"I was certainly born with one," the man chuckled. He turned and lead his men back the way they came.

"Any idea who them fellas was?" Morgan asked.

"Never seen them before," Skip shrugged.

"That was Duke Wilson," Alvarez said. "You are one lucky man, Amigo."

"Why do you say that?" Morgan asked.

"Wilson is a very bad man, Senor. He has killed many men and is utterly ruthless. I have never before heard of him backing down despite the odds being against him," Alvarez shook his head.

"So why you think he did this time?" Morgan asked. He knew Alvarez was a shrewd judge of men.

"He wanted to test the mettle of the men that ride for Senor Tillman. To see how much trouble we might make for him," Alvarez shrugged.

"Unless he starts it, I don't see how we would make any for him," Morgan replied. He pulled out the makings and rolled himself a smoke. He lit it and took a few puffs, thinking on what the Mexican had said.

"What do you think, Wade?" Skip asked.

"I think we need to push these cattle on down with the rest of the herd and let Mr. Tillman know about this," Morgan replied, spurring his horse into movement.

"Wade, you strike me as a man that's been down the trail some and seen the elephant. You think them men are gonna be trouble?" Skip asked him.

"I do. From what Mr. Tillman told me on the way out, Duke Wilson and his men have been playing hell in the area and nobody much seems inclined to do anything about it," Morgan puffed on his cigarette.

"They have at that. So far, they've left us alone for the most part. The Boss didn't expect that to last," Skip shook his head.

"Everybody willing to fight if it comes to that?" Morgan asked. He squeezed off his smoke and tossed it down.

"I suspect so. There might be one, maybe two I'm doubtful about," Skip nodded.

"Point them out to me when we get back," Morgan said.

"Why?" Skip asked.

"Cause it's down to the cutting. Root hog or die. If they ain't willing, then they ain't staying. I don't want nobody at my back I can't count on," Morgan replied, his tone cold and hard.

"I reckon you're right," Skip nodded.

"You know I am," Morgan replied.

The Masked Rider made his way back to Midnight. He was sure that Duke Wilson still had spies in town, for it was a better than even bet that he knew that two of his men had been gunned down by Wade Morgan, the newest hand to sign on the Double D ranch. That was one reason why Wilson had braced him on the range, to get a feel for the unknown gunslinger that had killed two of his men.

Mounting up he headed for the small cottage on the outside of town that belonged to the shop-keeper, Rufus Moore. If Moore's daughter was a hostage it might be a good idea to enroll his help in figuring out who in town that Duke Wilson was working with. Because The Masked Rider was sure that someone was.

Rufus Moore was asleep when the knock summoned him to his front door. Nobody was more surprised than Moore when he saw the masked man standing there, a cape folded around him. Moore wondered if there were guns beneath the cape, but knew better than to ask.

"Rufus Moore. Duke Wilson has your daughter captive," the masked man said.

"He does," Moore held his head submissively.

"Do you want her set free?" the masked man looked at him.

"I do," Moore said honestly.

"Perhaps you know why she was taken?" The masked man looked at him.

"She was taken to cow the Sheriff. He's in love with her," Moore replied.

"That explains a lot," the masked man nodded. "She'll be home soon," he said and then was vanished into the night. Rufus Moore looked at the doorway at the darkness for a long time…

⚜

Three of Duke Wilson's men were holed up in a small house on the outskirts of town. Joe Nelson threw another log on the fire. He was getting damned tired of all this waiting around. Duke had something planned, but the boss was playing his cards damned close to the vest. Sure the money was good, but Nelson wanted some action.

Watching the town was boring as hell. Even if they had the town buffaloed, it still rankled him to be sitting around and doing nothing. He lit a cigar and tossed the match out in the street. Something moved in the shadows. Nelson squinted, trying to see more clearly when something came flying out of the darkness. It took him a minute to recognize it for what it was, a three stick bundle of dynamite tied together and the fuse sputtering down to the blasting caps. Nelson dived off the porch as the dynamite sailed through the open door into the house.

Hellfire and lightning filled the night as the three sticks of dynamite exploded. The house vanished as board and glass filled the air. Flames roared into the night. Joe Nelson scrabbled in the dirt and saw a man dressed in black. He drew his pistol only to see the flames of a muzzle blast fill his vision and he felt a hammer blow to his chest that rocked him backwards onto his back. Before his vision faded to darkness he saw a man in black standing over him, holding a smoking gun.

The Masked Rider was long gone before the first of the townspeople responded to the explosion on the edge of town. Sheriff Cole Norton made his way to the scene and when he saw the house that was burning a smile touched his lips for the first time in a long time. Somebody was taking the fight to Duke Wilson and his men. Someone not afraid of the outlaw leader and his band. He had a pretty good idea it was the masked man in black and he was glad of it. It kept him free and clear, and thus kept Lucy Moore out of danger.

Wade Morgan rode back to where Blue Hawk had made camp. The Yaqui was waiting on him as he rode back into the camp. The Indian watched silently as Morgan changed from the black-clad Masked Rider back to the guise of Wade Morgan.

"I found the outlaw camp," Blue Hawk announced as Morgan poured himself a cup of coffee.

"Glad to hear it. I was busy in town tonight," Morgan chuckled.

"I heard the boom," Blue Hawk nodded impassively.

"It was loud," Morgan chuckled.

"How you think Wilson will take it?" Blue Hawk looked at him.

"Not well," Morgan nodded, his face suddenly serious.

"You think he will come looking you?" Blue Hawk asked.

"I hope he will," Morgan smiled grimly.

"He will come," the Yaqui nodded sagely. "Any closer to figuring out what is going around Yellow Mesa?"

"Not yet, but I am getting there. I think Duke Wilson is either working with or for someone and they are expecting a big payoff of some sort," Morgan nodded.

"That fits with what I overheard," Blue Hawk nodded. "Two men met not far from camp. I followed Duke Wilson back to his camp."

"You did the right thing. We needed to know where the women were being held and now we do. Now we need to track down the mastermind behind the trouble on Yellow Mesa. If the men meet again, follow the man from town. Tonight, I'm going to take the battle to Duke Wilson," The Masked Rider smiled. It wasn't a pleasant sight, and suddenly Blue Hawk almost felt sorry for the outlaw band. Almost.

Wade Morgan rode out on Midnight, letting the black have its head till they were nearing the area where Duke Wilson and his men were holed up. He reined Midnight in and approached more cautiously. He carried a canvas sack with him full of dynamite and blasting caps. He had switched

"I found the outlaw camp,"
Blue Hawk announced.

from his boots to his moccasins and was moving soundlessly towards the outlaw encampment.

From what Blue Hawk had told him, the women were kept in the main building under Wilson's direct control. That meant that the other buildings were fair game. The Masked Rider smiled as he bound four sticks together and capped them with fuse. He struck a match, shielding the fire from below and touched it to the fuse which immediately sputtered to life. The Rider threw it at one of the smaller bunk houses and watched as it sailed through the night air to land on the roof. He lit a second bundle and sent another one sailing towards the corral. The first bundle detonated sending flames and wood flying as the one hit the corral and exploded, destroying the split rail fence. The spooked horses ran.

Men ran out of the bunkhouse and the Rider aimed his Winchester and dusted a few of the outlaws, dropping three before they realized they were even being shot at. One man ran for the privy and the Rider sent another bundle of dynamite sailing through the air. It hit at the back as the man ran through the door. The dynamite exploded as the methane trapped inside the outhouse ignited sending it rocketing into the air. The rider fired his rifle and the outlaw tumbled into the burning pit. Grinning, Morgan withdrew leaving the chaos burning in his wake…

Wade Morgan rode back in to the Double D at dawn. Cookie was already up and had coffee on. Morgan stopped and got him a cup of coffee and some breakfast.

"You have been up to some mischief," Cookie noted.

"I have. I reckon Duke Wilson didn't have a right peaceful night," Morgan chuckled.

"You figure he's gonna be on the prod today?" Cookie eyed him speculatively.

"He might. He lost a few men last night," Morgan allowed.

"Boss will be pleased to hear that when he wakes up," Cookie nodded.

"I reckon he might. You care to pass the news along? I plan on hitting the sheets and resting for a mite," Morgan told him as he polished off a plateful of steak and eggs and biscuits and gravy. He drank a second cup of coffee and smoked a cigarette. The sun was just beginning to rise as Morgan made his way to the bunkhouse. The other men were starting to stir as he rolled into his blankets and fell into a deep and restful sleep.

Duke Wilson charged out of the main house with a pistol in his hand into a scene straight out of Hell. Flames were leaping into the air, bathing everything in a hellish glow. Gunshots rang out and Wilson saw two of his men fall. Four more were scattered about the yard with long pieces of wood impaling their bodies, shards of the cabin he guessed. Suddenly the other cabin exploded and the air was full of flying splinters and shards of glass as well as body parts. A hand hit his shoulder and tumbled off to the ground.

Hardened criminal that he was, that was more than even Duke Wilson could take and he vomited. As his head snapped forward another rifle shot rang out and his hat flew from his head. Duke Wilson dove for the dirt, landing in the supper he had just lost and cussing a blue streak. More men fell as bullets found them. Wilson's gun was in his hand and he was shooting at shadows just like his men.

Finally the shooting stopped and there were only the screams and cries of the wounded and the crackling of flames in the burning shacks. Duke Wilson climbed out of the dirt and vomit, his face a mask of rage. Someone had made a mockery of him, had defied him! That was not something he would let pass. The people of Clanton's Folly would pay for what had happened this night. Duke Wilson swore it!

───

Lucy Moore and Claudia Chapman were thrown from their beds by the explosions. The two young women held each other as they watched through the windows as men died outside. Someone was finally carrying the fight to the outlaws and Lucy was glad to see it. For too long, Duke Wilson had run roughshod over the people of Clanton's Folly and the surrounding ranches.

It tore at her that Cole had not stood up to the outlaws after they had taken her, but at the same time she could not find fault with the man that she loved. She knew that she was the reason that the sheriff had knuckled under to the outlaws. She was surprised by her father's reticence to deal with it though.

Suddenly the door flew open and Duke Wilson stomped into the room, stinking of smoke and vomit, the outlaw grabbed Claudia Chapman and dragged her out of the cabin. Lucy flinched as she watched Duke Wilson slap Claudia off her feet. Tears filled her eyes as she saw Claudia hit the dirt. She realized that Claudia would be an example to the townspeople.

Lucy closed her eyes and covered her ears, not wanting to hear the cries of her friend as Duke Wilson brutalized her. She knew that Claudia would be used and used badly. The survivors of this night would do as they pleased to get back at the townspeople. Lucy shivered knowing that they might come for her as well.

It seemed like an eternity before the door opened and Claudia was shoved roughly inside. The naked girl curled into a fetal ball, crying and making high-pitched mewling noises. Blood stained her thighs. The door was pulled shut and a bar was thrown across the door from the outside locking the two women in. Lucy went to Claudia immediately and covered her with a blanket and then helped her over to her bed. Almost mechanically Lucy went to the washbasin and wet a wash cloth then wrung it out then walked over to Claudia and began to clean her up, making soothing noises to try and calm her friend. Lucy knew in her heart that Duke Wilson would do the same to her if he took a notion.

Duke Wilson gathered his surviving men together in the main cabin and sat them down. He looked them over and smiled at the evil-looking crew. They had been with him for years, since the end of the war, raping and pillaging their way across the west.

"We've waited long enough. This here tonight was the last straw. I want five of you to ride into town today and get the others. We'll hit the mine tonight and the bank at sunrise and burn that damned town to the ground," Wilson told them. He rolled a smoke and lit it, blowing out a cloud of smoke.

"Who you want to go, Duke?" Blackjack Carson asked. Carson was a big, heavy shouldered man with a long shaggy beard and a squinty eye.

"You take Blue, Link, Cuddy, Davis and Cletus with you. Round up Joe and the others and find out what's been going on around town. I want a full report when the rest of us get to town tonight," Wilson replied.

"C'mon boys, let's ride for town," Blackjack roared. The designated men stood and followed him out the door. Duke Wilson watched them go, frowning. Blackjack seemed to be getting big for his britches. It might be time to get rid of him. Wilson turned back to the rest of his men.

⁓⊚ ⊚⁓

Wade Morgan woke up to Tillman standing over his bunk grinning. "I heard you played hob last night," Tillman said.

"I certainly tried. What time is it?" Morgan asked, blinking at the bright sunlight.

"Cookie's fixing lunch if you feel like eating. Rest of the boys will be riding in soon. You figure on joining on the meal?" Tillman was still grinning.

"Soon's I'm washed up and dressed boss," Morgan grinned back. Tillman chuckled and headed out of the bunkhouse. Morgan was surprised that the rancher had let him sleep so long. Tillman wasn't the sort to let a man rest if he was earning a working wage. It set him to wondering if maybe he wasn't barking up the wrong tree.

Wade Morgan usually was not a man given to introspection, but for some reason, this day, he was. The man he had once been was dead and buried along with his family on a hard-scrabble farm in western Missouri. He could easily have ridden off into the high lonesome once he had recovered from his wounds, never to be heard from again. But he had not been able to do that. Not as long as the killers of his family rode free. So instead he had changed his name, practiced with his guns until he never missed no matter how hurried the shot. He had donned the black costume and mask of the Masked Rider, bringing justice to those who could not get it for themselves.

Some called his alter ego a criminal, a cold-blooded killer of the worst sort. Many men had gone down before his guns and died, but many lives had been saved because of those same guns as well. He had no regrets about the path he had chosen. Many had asked how a masked man could stand for Justice, but those who he had saved knew the answer to that question. Of them all, only Blue Hawk knew any of his secrets. For the Yaqui had found him and nursed him back to health.

Blue Hawk had saved his life and he owed the Yaqui more than he would ever care to admit. Just as Morgan had saved Blue Hawk's life on more than one occasion. The Indian was his closest and only friend. The two of them had been together for years as they had travelled the west, rooting out outlaws and cleaning up towns that needed help to rid themselves of a violent criminal element. Clanton's Folly was such a town, held hostage by Duke Wilson and his men.

The plight of the two young women troubled Wade Morgan immensely. Nobody but the worst sort of trash messed with a western woman, because that was the surest way to get strung up or maybe worse. If anything happened to those two young women, Duke Wilson would die, and in a manner that might well make a Comanche or even an Apache puke! The Masked Rider would see to it. Normally, he was a fair if hard man. But crimes against women were the foulest of all, and given what had been done to his wife and children.

Wade Morgan took a deep breath and let it out slowly. He could not allow himself to think about that. No better he concentrate on a plan to rescue the two women. They needed his help in the worst possible way, but he had to act in such a manner as to not blow the cover he had established in and around Clanton's Folly.   He couldn't risk anyone finding out he was the Masked Rider, for if that were to happen, he would have to find a new identity and lay the Wade Morgan identity to rest for good. He wasn't ready to do that.

The Masked Rider liked the persona of the easy going cowhand. It was a welcome relief from the high-pressure identity of the Masked Rider. Morgan sipped from a cup of coffee before heading for his horse. "I'm going to check those canyons just north of the west range," Wade Morgan announced as he stepped into the saddle.

"You want to take anybody with you?" Sam Tillman looked at him. The ranch owner seemed surprised at the declaration.

"Sure, can I'll Take Alverez and Skip," Morgan replied laconically.

"Good men," Tillman acknowledged.

"They are," Morgan agreed.

"You like having things your way don't you?" Tillman looked at him.

"I do," Morgan nodded.

"You sure like to take your chances, don't you?" Skip shook his head as the three men rode out from the ranch.

"I do," Wade Morgan grinned.

"You really expect to win this?" Skip asked.

"I do," Wade grinned.

"How?" Skip looked at him.

"The hard way," Wade smiled back.

"I ain't sure that buckin' the Boss is the way to do it," Skip shook his head.

"That what it looked like?" Wade grinned.

"It did," Alvarez agreed.

"Would it surprise you to know that's what him and me wanted it to look like?" Wade asked casually as they rode.

"Why would you do that?" Skip asked, scratching his head.

"Because there is a spy at the Double D working for Duke Wilson," Wade replied, spurring his horse ahead and leaving the two hands to chew on that for a few minutes.

It didn't take long for them to catch up to him full of questions and fighting mad at the idea that there was a rider among them that wasn't riding for the brand! "Any idea who the spy is?" Skip demanded as he rode up.

"Not by name, no," Wade replied, building himself a smoke. He got the quirly rolled and struck a match on the saddle horn and fired it up.

"How do you know then?" Alverez asked from his other side.

"He woke me up coming in the other night. The next day we braced Duke Wilson on Double D land," Wade shrugged, exhaling smoke through his nostrils like an angry bull.

"What do you figure Wilson is after, anyway?" Skip asked. The young cowhand had a quick mind and was a lot smarter than he let on, Morgan observed.

"Best guess is the gold shipment and payroll for the mine. From what the boss told me, they been stockpiling a while, even before Duke Wilson rode into the territory. What I'm wondering is who sent for Wilson," Morgan replied.

"That question, if answered, might solve all the trouble around Yellow Mesa and Clanton's Folly," Alverez said thoughtfully. The Mexican wrangler was building a smoke of his own and receded into his thoughts.

"Wade, you really think that there is somebody behind Duke Wilson?" Skip asked, looking at him.

"I do. Wilson never hits unless it is a sure thing. He has to be getting inside information," Wade Morgan replied.

"Only way to explain his success," Skip nodded.

"I trust you two and the boss. Period. I think we're likely gonna run into Wilson or at least some of his men today. I gotta know now if you have the sand to stand and fight if it comes down to the nut-cutting?" Morgan told them both.

"We'll back your play," Skip replied looking at Alverez who nodded his agreement.

"Good. It might get mighty dicey out there today. Be ready for anything and keep your guns loose and ready. Now, boys, we got us some cattle to round up!" Morgan grinned, spurring his horse into a run.

Snoots McCoy frowned as he looked out over the valley. Below, three men had gathered about a hundred head of cattle. McCoy looked to his left and right. "Scatter the cattle and kill them cowboys," McCoy ordered his men. Duke Wilson had told him to hit the Double D hard!

The five outlaws charged down the hill, pistols firing and whooping and hollering as they rode! McCoy was in the front so it really wasn't a surprise when he caught the first bullet from below! McCoy tumbled from the saddle as the other riders swept down the hill. None of the others noticed that he was gone.

Wade Morgan had spotted the riders and drew the Winchester from its boot on his saddle and jacked a round into the chamber. When they started their charge down the hill, he lifted his rifle and fired, knocking one of the riders out of the saddle. He worked the lever and fired again as Skip and Alverez entered the dance. In a matter of seconds the saddles of the charging horses were empty. "Let's get these cattle calmed down," Morgan called.

He gave no more thought to the raiders. They were dead or soon would be. Skip and the Mexican didn't miss, not anymore than he did. The important thing at the moment was the round up. Anything else would follow once that was done.

Getting ready for a trail drive was big business for most outfits. For the Double D it was no different. If they couldn't get the cattle to market, they would lose money and without money they couldn't afford to pay their bills or their hands. And men that didn't get paid were less than willing to work.

Morgan knew how important it was to get the cattle branded and get them to market. Those cattle would provide working capital for the Double D for the next year. Getting them branded and ready for market was necessary if the ranch and the brand were to survive.

Within 24 hours they had gathered and branded more than 200 head of cattle. "Let's get them headed back to the main ranch," Morgan said.

"Sounds like a plan," Skip agreed.

"Wilson's men failed. We need to make sure that continues," Morgan said.

"I just want to get my hands on that spy. I don't cotton to working with no traitor," Skip said, squaring himself in the saddle. Morgan couldn't contain a grin. The boy had plenty of sand and he'd do to ride the river with any time!

***

"Boss, Snook and them others never come back," Luke Strickland carried the news to Duke Wilson.

"I reckon by now they probably won't. The Double D is proving a tougher nut to crack than we thought. Get a bunch together and go see what you can do about it Luke. It's time we showed this damn town who's the boss!" Wilson replied.

Luke Strickland was grinning as he headed at the door. He knew a few of the gang who were salty enough to ride roughshod on that ranch. It would be like a ride in the park!

***

Blue Feather stood in the general store in Clanton's Folly. The Yaqui waited patiently as Rufus Moore filled his order for supplies. "Town quiet," Blue Feather observed.

"That's the way we like it," Moore said, his disdain for the Indian evident in both his glare and his tone.

"Quiet good," Blue Feather nodded.

"It is. That will be twenty dollars," Moore said after he had filled the bag.

"Price steep," Blue Feather met his gaze. The Yaqui's eyes were cold and hard as rocks.

"You don't like it, go somewhere else," Moore smiled nastily.

Blue Feather dropped a Double Eagle on the counter and picked up the bag and carried it out of the store. He had taken an instant dislike to the store-keeper and he had been able to sense that the feeling was mutual. Prejudice was something that the Yaqui had faced many times in the past and knew he would face again. Most white men thought of Indians as ignorant savages. Most of them never had a clue.

Blue Feather came from a long line of warriors. He had learned the ways of the warrior before he had reached ten summers. He had grown up in a harsh desert environment where survival was a day to day thing. The way of the Indian and the way of the white man were vastly different. Most whites felt that the stoic Indian was a fearsome savage. They knew next to nothing of his sense of humor or of his beliefs. No, they were too wrapped up in themselves to understand the starry path or the will of Man Above. He shook his head.

Tom Voorhees looked over at Sam Champlain. "You think Duke Wilson is really in Clanton's Folly?"

"There or someplace close by," Sam Champlain replied. Champlain was a bounty hunter.

"You figure the Masked Rider is around too?" Tom asked.

"Duke Wilson is too big for him not to go after him. Both of them carry big bounties on their head," Champlain shrugged.

"Not everyone believes the Rider is a crook. He has a lot of support on high," Tom looked at his partner.

"You sound like an admirer."

"Man does a lot of good; some of it is outside the law, Sam."

"Makes him an outlaw Tom. No if ands or buts about it."

"You've been wrong before, Sam."

"I have."

"I think you are again where the Masked Rider is concerned, Sam."

"You really want to argue the point, Tom?" Sam Champlain asked.

"No, but it is what I believe," Tom Voorhees countered.

"Tom, you got a lot to learn," Champlain shook his head.

Wade Morgan was riding drag. Skip and Alverez were up ahead guiding the herd towards the gather. He had pulled a bandana up over his face to make it easier to breathe through the dust that the herd was kicking up. His eyes also roamed the hills, ever alert for trouble. With luck, he would be able to rendezvous with Blue Hawk and see what the Yaqui had managed to find in town.

The rumors of Duke Wilson being in the area would soon draw the attention of others. Others that Wade Morgan really didn't want digging around. The Masked Rider had a reputation as an outlaw, and as such he was a target for bounty hunters. Some of them had gotten close over the years. That was not something that Wade Morgan wanted to deal with at the moment.

The cows were moving quickly and it wasn't long until they ran into some of the other hands with about another hundred or so head. Morgan reined to a halt and watched as the two bunches were blended into one larger herd. More would be joining them soon enough when they gathered them in the pasture near the ranch house. Oddly, Morgan felt himself smiling. This was what he missed the most. The camaraderie of the bunkhouse; watching a herd grow and then move out as the drive to market started. The life of the Masked Rider was a lonely one. However it was a job that needed doing.

The criminals that preyed on the weak, the innocent, and the defenseless needed to be hunted down and put out of business so that the west could continue to grow. Morgan pulled out the makings and rolled himself a quirly. A match was struck on the saddle horn and the flame touched to the end of his hand-rolled cigarette. Once it was going good he shook the flame out and crushed the burnt end of the match on the saddle to horn to make sure it was out before discarding it. He had no desire to be the cause of a prairie fire.

Morgan pulled aside his bandana and puffed on his smoke as he watched the herd mill. His eyes scanned the hills around, searching for anything out of place. Trouble was coming. He could smell it on the wind. Duke Wilson's men were up there somewhere, watching the gather, getting ready to make their move. Morgan had fronted Wilson, made him back down. It

Trouble was coming. He could smell it on the wind.

wasn't something that the outlaw could let pass without retaliation.

Not to mention the fun he had with the dynamite at the outlaw camp. Wilson wouldn't know it was him in his other guise as the Black Rider, but he would suspect Wade Morgan as being behind it. It would push Wilson into a corner. The outlaw king would have to strike back and that strike would be ruthless.

Wilson would not let it rest. He couldn't and keep the respect of his gang. He had to strike back, and when he did, Wade Morgan had to be ready; ready to repel the attack and to take no prisoners.

Luke Strickland lowered the spyglass. He had watched as the two herds had merged on their way down out of the hills. His job, as he understood it from Duke Wilson was to scatter that heard to hell and gone, killing as many of the hands as possible while doing so. He reined in his horse and gently turned her back into the woods. He had some planning to do.

"Boss," Morgan swung down out of the saddle. Sam Tillman nodded his greeting.

"Looks like you rounded up a good bunch," Tillman said.

"More out there too, but I got to doing some thinking and figured we needed to talk."

"I figured the same thing, Frank Hollars over at the mine sent word that he can't wait no longer, he's got to ship the ore out."

"That will draw Wilson out for sure. Thing is we gotta be ready when he fixes to strike. I've backed him down and he can't let that go and keep his reputation. He's gonna send a force in here to disrupt or destroy the round-up," Morgan explained.

"You seem pretty sure of that," Tillman observed.

"I am. Spotted some of his men watching from the hills as we merged the herd," Wade Morgan confided.

"Son of a bitch! When you figure they'll hit?" Tillman looked at him.

"More than likely after we've bedded down for the night. Their man will volunteer for Nighthawk duty and tip them when to attack. I figure they'll try to stampede the herd right through the camp and kill everybody that way," Morgan replied, his eyes still scanning the hills. He knew the enemy was up there, waiting.

Morgan wished he could get word to Blue Hawk. The Yaqui could be a big help, acting as both scout and lookout for the cowboys working the round-up. Of course, the intelligence he was gathering in town would also be helpful; once Morgan got a chance to hear of it. That was the bad part about working undercover.

Circumstances sometimes prevented the sharing of gathered intelligence, which could lead to problems. It was a lesson he had learned during the War Between the States. Morgan felt an itch between his shoulder blades and turned suddenly. One cowhand that had been less than friendly turned away suddenly, like he had been caught reaching into the cook's pie without an invitation. Wade Morgan smiled. He had identified the spy in the camp.

Blue Hawk drifted out of town. He had much to think about and to tell the Masked Rider. Duke Wilson did have a spy in town and he had been very surprised to learn who that inside man was. He shook his head, knowing that greed did strange things to a man. It was a white man's concept and one he would never understand.

Blue Hawk shook his head. He would ride to the ranch where Morgan worked and ask for a job. It would be for the best, and it would also allow him and Morgan a chance to talk!

It was late in the day when one of the men rode up to Morgan. "Rider coming," the man said.

"Thanks," Morgan replied, riding out to meet the rider. He had already recognized Blue Hawk from the distance and was glad to see him. "Hello, my friend," Morgan greeted his faithful Indian companion.

"Amigo, I bring news from town," Blue Hawk replied.

"Tell me."

"Store owner is in cahoots with Wilson. Saw him send message through one of Wilson's men in town about mine. Thought you should know," Blue Hawk explained.

"It explains a lot, Blue Hawk. How would you feel about scouting and night-hawking for this bunch? I'm expecting trouble tonight and could use an extra hand," Morgan asked.

"Understood, Amigo," the Yaqui grinned.

"Follow me then," Morgan ordered as he turned his horse and rode back to Sam Tillman. "This is Blue Hawk. I've rode with him before and he's a helluva a scout and look out. I want him to ride Nighthawk tonight."

"You ain't done wrong by me yet, so I reckon I'll let you continue to play out your string," Tillman nodded. Morgan nodded and went to introduce Blue Hawk to the rest of the boys. Only one man seemed upset about the Yaqui riding the night watch. It was the same fellow that Morgan had caught giving him unfriendly looks.

⁂

Frank Hollars ran his fingers through his hair. The men were getting ready to revolt if they didn't get paid soon. Duke Wilson be damned, he had to get the gold shipment out! It'd be nice if the damned Town Sheriff had some balls!

Wilson and his crowd had been why he had kept delaying the shipment. It wasn't a coincidence that they hadn't struck before now. Other than the kidnapping of the two women to quell one of the ranchers and the Sheriff. Nobody said anything, but they all knew. Hollars shook his head, wishing he had someway of getting outside help in. But Wilson's men had Yellow Mesa sewn up tight.

⁂

Duke Wilson walked into the cabin, eyeing the two women. The Moore girl glared defiantly at him despite the fact that the other girl lay lifelessly on the bed, her eyes clouded and glazed over despite the fact that she still breathed. Wilson knew the look, her mind was gone, shattered by what his men had done to her. He cared neither one way or the other.

"She lives?" he asked Lucy Moore.

"Barely," Lucy hissed, her contempt for the outlaw and his men palpable. Claudia Chapman was more dead than alive, trapped inside her own mind with the horrors that she had experienced.

"You remember that if more trouble hits. You'll be next," Wilson smirked at her.

"If I get the chance, Duke Wilson, I'll cut your heart out of your chest and dine on it like an Apache," Lucy glared at the outlaw king.

"I believe you would," Wilson laughed. But he was also wary for he believed that Lucy Moore would do exactly what she had said given the opportunity.

⁂

It was two o'clock in the morning as Luke Strickland and his men made their way down to the herd. They had spent a big part of the day watching cows being branded even as more cows came along. To Strickland's way of thinking, they could spook the heard and drive them through camp with little too worry about.

He spread his men out, all of them waiting for his signal. Luke Strickland smiled as he thought of the Double D hands dying under the hooves of the stampeding cattle. It would make the boss very happy! Duke Wilson was pretty sure that the Double D was behind the troubles that had suddenly hit the outlaw camp. Wilson was pretty sure the new hand; Wade Morgan had played a big part in it. Luke Strickland lifted his Colt in the air and fired, his men responding in kind and soon the entire herd of cattle was running towards the camp where the Double D hands lay sleeping!

※ ◎

Except none of the Double D hands were asleep and they were waiting for the stampede to happen. At the first shot, the hands from the Double D were circling around behind the rustlers. Wade Morgan was looking for one man in particular because that man had sold out his fellow cowhands. He had betrayed the greatest trust by selling out his friends and his boss. When you signed on, you agreed to ride for the brand! Anyone who broke that promise could expect nothing more than a bullet from their coworkers.

※ ◎

As the raiders started forward, firing their guns, the hands from the Double D had worked their way behind them and Wade Morgan opened the dance! His Winchester belched fire and lead and he was working the lever, spinning the rifle and roll-cocking it before the sound of the first shot died away! Strickland and his men hit the ground quick, some from bullets others from their horses racing into the stampede of spooked cattle and falling, meeting the fate they had intended for the hands of the Double D.

Once the rustler's saddles had been cleared, Wade Morgan started yelling orders and the cowhands went to work to head off the stampede. Morgan didn't intend to lose any of Tillman's cattle that had been rounded up. Once they got the herd milling and resettled, he planned to take the fight to Duke Wilson and finish it. The rest of the hands could find any missing cows come the dawn.

"You called it right, Morgan," Sam Tillman rode up.

"Wilson is pretty predictable. Once we get the herd settled, Blue Hawk and I are going after Duke Wilson. He'll be setting up for the shipment of gold ore from the mines. I want to be ready when he goes for it so we can end this," Morgan explained.

"Sounds like a plan. You sure you don't want to take a few of the boys with you?"

"You need 'em here, Sam. Come daylight you're gonna have to send some of these boys searching for strays. I don't aim for you to lose a single cow out of this gather."

"That's not too realistic a goal, Morgan."

"Maybe not, but you already lost a hand, cause he was in with the rustlers. Keeping all you cows seems like a good goal," Morgan took out the makings and built himself a smoke.

"I appreciate it. You saved me a lot of grief this night, not to mention my life. I'm not sure what I can do to repay that," Tillman shook his head.

"Don't worry about it Sam. Let me collect Blue Hawk and we'll take care of the rest," Morgan smiled as he exhaled smoke.

"I get the feeling that you and that Injun have worked together before," Tillman looked at him.

"You'd be right. Okay, Sam, I need to go. It's time to end this," Morgan nodded, urging his horse towards the herd.

Duke Wilson had gathered the rest of his men. Word had come from town that the gold shipment was going out at daylight. Wilson smiled. He was glad, wanting nothing more than to have this town behind him. Bad luck had dogged him since he arrived here and Duke Wilson was a superstitious man. The men getting killed by a saddle tramp had been the first bad omen, the bombing of his camp another. He wondered how much of it was the fault of Rufus Moore's daughter, his hostage to keep the sheriff in line.

His bad luck had seemed to start once he had taken the two women hostage. When his men rode out, he was going to leave both the women behind. It would take them at least a week to walk back to town and he and his men would be long gone by that time. Wilson smiled at the thought.

Wade Morgan had donned the guise of The Masked Rider after he and Blue Hawk had left the cattle camp and he rode astride Midnight now. The Black was eager for action and Morgan wasn't entirely sure that he blamed him. His involvement as Wade Morgan had precluded his spending time in the skin he was far more accustomed too, that of The Masked Rider. He had ridden the area in both guises and had a pretty good idea of where Duke Wilson would set his ambush for the gold shipment. The key would be getting into place and remaining unseen as Wilson set up his ambush. Only then would he be able to ambush the ambusher.

Duke Wilson was angry. His mind was on his silent partner, the one who had summoned him to Yellow Mesa. He had a lot to answer for. If nothing else happened, he would settle up with the man. Settle up with lead! He had left the women tied up; figuring if they didn't get loose it was their own damn fault!

Still, he wanted that gold shipment. Wanted it bad. It would be the biggest haul of his career. Wade Morgan. Wilson frowned as he thought of the drifting cowhand who had so totally disrupted his plans.

"Get into place," Wilson yelled at his men. The sun hadn't risen quite yet.

"We're ready Boss," one of the men yelled back. Wilson shot him a dirty look. Sound would carry far in the canyon. Wilson wanted to take the wagon by surprise, something he was growing more and more unsure of.

≈⊚ ⊚≈

Lucy Moore struggled against the ropes. She had managed to get her hands in front of her and was worrying the hemp with her teeth. Fortunately her teeth were strong. Poor Claudia hadn't spoken, had barely even moved since the outlaw gang had taken her and used her. Lucy breathed a prayer of thanks that she had been spared from that particular fate. Deep down, part of her wondered why?

The only obvious answer was that she had been more valuable to Duke Wilson than Claudia. Why was that? Her relationship with Cole Norton? Or something else? Something more sinister? Lucy pushed the thoughts out of her head and went back to work gnawing at the rope.

≈⊚ ⊚≈

The mastermind behind the whole affair was sitting astride his horse a few miles out of town. He had taken a ride to clear his head. So much was riding on the gold shipment and on if Duke Wilson could pull the robbery off. He hadn't liked having to bring the outlaw in, but there had been no other choice that he had been able to find. He and Wilson had fought side by side in the War Between the States. Wilson was the only person he could trust to help him pull this off. Once it was done, they would both be set for life.

He put his boots to the horse, turning and heading it back towards town. The sun would be up soon, and it would be better if he was back in town when word of the robbery arrived. Cole Norton would raise a posse, but they would be ineffective, because of the leverage he made sure that they would have against the Sheriff.

≈⊚ ⊚≈

Cole Norton stood on the boardwalk in front of the jail. The mine was sending out a shipment of gold at sunrise. It was what Duke Wilson had been waiting for. It was why Lucy and Claudia had been taken. It was why he had been acting like a whipped dog for the past month. Cole Norton had put down the whiskey after his visit from the masked man and hadn't touched it since. For the first time in a while he was thinking clearly and his hands were steady.

His horse was saddled and ready and Cole Norton climbed into the saddle. He planned to escort that Gold Shipment out of Clanton's Folly to Santa Fe. If Wilson tried to hit it, he planned on gunning the outlaw down like a mad dog.

Duke Wilson had his men set up for the ambush. They would take the gold before it ever reached Clanton's Folly. In fact they planned on taking it on the trail from the Mine into town. Wilson figured it would be simpler that way.

He was still stinging from the fact that Strickland and his crew had never returned from their assault on the Double D ranch. He figured that they were probably dead by this time. Otherwise they would have returned. Which meant that Wade Morgan had out-maneuvered him again. Wilson frowned at the thought of the cowboy that had backed him down. Nobody had ever done that before. It was not something that he could let pass, even if he had to call Morgan out in the streets of Clanton's Folly. So far he had been forced to let it ride, but soon that would no long be necessary. Not after they had the gold shipment.

Frank Hollars watched the sun start to rise over the horizon. He waved his arm and the two wagons bearing the gold ore headed out, on the trail to Santa Fe. His mine was one of the richest in the New Mexico territory and he hated the fact that Duke Wilson was in the area. The outlaw had made a helluva name for himself.

Hollars had a bad feeling about this for a long time, ever since Wilson had shown up in the area. Cole Norton had become as worthless as tits on a bull. Frank Hollars shook his head. He hoped that Sam Tillman was right about that young fella he had hired on.

The Masked Rider crouched on a rock above the trail. He could see all of Wilson's men. Blue Hawk was beside him. The Yaqui had a brand new Winchester leveled at the robbers as did the Rider himself. The Masked Rider also had a few blasting caps ready and waiting. He built himself a smoke and fired it up.

Lucy Moore shook the rope from her wrists, and went to work untying her ankles. It too a few minutes before she had Claudia free as well. The young woman didn't even open her eyes as Lucy freed her from her bonds. When she did open them, they were empty and lifeless. Lucy fought back tears for her friend.

The two wagons rumbled down the trail towards Clanton's folly. Sheriff Cole Norton was riding out to meet them as Outlaws opened fire, killing the guards riding along side. Duke Wilson stepped out in front of the wagons, a double barreled shotgun clenched in his fists.

"Get off the stage," Wilson commanded. The Driver looked at him. Just then bullets began to strike the outlaw band, driving riders from their saddles never to sit them again. The Driver had the right idea and set the wagon back in motion, cracking the whip and sending it towards Clanton's Folly as fast as the horses drawing the wagons would go!

The Masked Rider and Blue Hawk gunned down the outlaws in short order. Duke Wilson hit the dirt along with the rest, a .44 bullet stopping his heart. Blue Hawk looked over him. "Are we done?"

"Not yet. You go free the women, I am going to face down the man behind it all," The Masked Rider announced.

"Yes, Amigo," Blue Hawk nodded, riding off towards the outlaws hide-out.

The Masked Rider headed for town. He knew exactly where to go and who to confront once he got there. He had a good idea that Sheriff Cole Norton would have figured who was behind it all by now as well.

Rufus Moore looked out the window as a black-clad and masked rider rode up the street. He was shocked; he had thought that the man was only a legend, a ghost or myth spread by those who didn't know. The masked man reigned up in front of his store and slid out of the saddle.

"Who are you," Rufus asked.

"I am the Masked Rider. Rufus Moore, you are a villain of the worst kind. You were willing to sacrifice your own daughter for gold. It is time for you to pay," The Rider said. The store owner went for his gun and the Rider's spoke first. It was finally over and Yellow Mesa was safe once more.

Epilogue

Cole Norton had kicked his horse into a gallop as the sound of gunfire reached him. Then he heard the roar of express guns and more shooting and the gunfire faded as he drew nearer to the source. Two wagons rumbled into view and he recognized them as belonging to the mine. Frank Hollars was on the lead wagon along with Dusty Barnes and Danny Poe. Hollars was driving the wagon and the other two men were riding guard. Norton waved them down, making sure they could see his badge.

"What the hell was happenin' back there?" Norton asked.

"Duke Wilson and his boys tried to get the gold, what they got was dead," Hollars chuckled.

"How?" Norton was stunned.

"We had a couple of guardian angels up in the rocks that evened the odds and helped us win the day. Saw some of Tillman's boys from the Double D heading that way as well, figured they mop up what was left," Hollars fired up a cigar and looked happier than Norton could ever remember seeing him. Norton spurred his horse onward, a feeling of dread washing over him. He had to find Lucy!

Cole Norton had no trouble back-tracking Wilson's gang to their hideout. He shook his head when he saw the bombed out outbuildings. Only one building was untouched. Norton pulled his Winchester from the saddle boot as he climbed down from his horse and worked the lever, chambering a round. There were noises coming from the still standing cabin. Cautiously he approached and threw open the door. "Lucy!" he cried spotting the young woman that he loved as she struggled with her bonds. After making sure none of Wilson's men were still lurking about he drew his knife and cut the ropes and drew Lucy Moore into his arms. They held each other for a long time.

※ ☙

Two days had passed since Cole Norton had ridden back into two in a wagon carrying Lucy More and Claudia Chapman, his horse tied behind it. It was only when they returned to town that they learned what had happened to Rufus Moore. Among his papers were letters exchanged between Moore and Wilson, plotting their taking of Clanton's Folly.

Lucy had clung tightly to Cole, her eyes filled with tears and wondering why. That was an answer Norton could never give her because it had gone with Rufus Moore to the grave. However in the past two days, Norton had done some asking around. The young cowhand Wade Morgan was gone, vanished from the territory as if he had never been.

Cole also gave a lot of thought to the black clad masked man who had forced him to see himself through the eyes of the town, but then had seen something more below the surface. He had reawakened Cole's self-respect, and that was a debt he would owe the man forever. He knocked on Lucy's door. Her father had left her a comfortable inheritance and with careful investment, could be made to grow.

"Thanks for coming, Cole," Lucy smile wanly as she opened the door. Norton removed his hat.

"Thanks for inviting me, Lucy. How are you feeling?" Cole Norton was genuinely concerned.

"As well as could be expected, all things considered. I went over to the Doctor's to visit with Claudia. She's no better."

"What did Doc have to say about it?" Cole's voice was soft and comforting.

"Claudia may never recover. She's retreated into herself. Her father is planning on sending her back east to a sanitarium for treatment. Cole, did you know who killed my father?" Eye blue eyes were wide.

"I think so, Lucy. Your father was killed in the name of justice by a man known across the west as the Masked Rider," Cole whispered. He kept his own thoughts concerning the Masked Rider's identity to himself.

"Cole, do you still want to marry me?" Lucy asked.

"I do," Cole replied. Tears spilled from her eyes and Lucy threw herself into his arms yet again, only this time it was for the best reason of all: love.

THE END

Thoughts on the Old West & the Men Who Brought Justice to it...

When I first connected with Airship 27, Ron Fortier asked me what I would be interested working on and I asked, "Got anything set in the Old West?" Ron just grinned and sent me the material on a western avenger called The Masked Rider.

I grew up on the Lone Ranger, Gunsmoke, Bonanza, Have Gun Will Travel to name a few, so I thought, *okay I can do this.* So I looked back at what made those old shows so great. There was always a pretty vile villain that was robbing and killing and needed to be brought to justice. My next question was what the villain has done that is keeping the town marshal at bay?

I quickly went to work, having Wade Morgan arrive in the town of Clanton's Folly in the shadow of Yellow Mesa. Vultures of Yellow Mesa is more a Wade Morgan story than a Masked Rider story, at least because Morgan is much more involved in the action, but it gave me a chance to look deeper into the man that is the Masked Rider and what motivates him.

What followed was a fun and hopefully engaging western romp not seen since Clayton Moore last graced the small screen as The Lone Ranger. It is a story that I hope will convey my personal love of the west and the men and women who built this country through their fortitude and desire to make America grow.

BILL CRAIG - author of The Jack Riley Adventures: *Valley of Death, Mayan Gold, Dead Run, Pirate's Blood, The Child Stealers,* and *The Mummy's Tomb*; as well as, The Fantastic Adventures of Hard-luck Hannigan: *Emerald Death, The Sky Masters, River of The Sun, Ghosts of the Sargasso, Curse of the Kill Devil* and *The Spear of Goliath.* Plus the Sam Decker Mysteries: *Scorpion Cay, Killshot* and *Decker P.I: Death Song.* And the Noir suspense thriller *The Butterfly Tattoo.* Contributor to the weird western anthology *Six Guns straight from Hell.* http://billcraig.webs.com/

THE MASKED RIDER

"The Hunting Party"

by Roman Leary

It wasn't a cave so much as a shallow recess between the rocks, but it was deep enough to conceal the old man and the little girl. They huddled there in the cool darkness, waiting for death.

It would come sooner for the old man. The bullet in his side had seen to that. The flow of blood was slow and steady and black. He kept a hand pressed to the wound in a futile attempt to stall the inevitable. He felt stupid for doing it. What was the point? Maybe it would be better to just let the life run out, to join his murdered son and daughter-in-law in whatever world awaited him. Maybe...

His grand-daughter stirred against him, and whimpered. He held her tighter with his free hand, pulled her closer to him. He felt her heartbeat through his coat, and the butterfly pulse of it drove away his thoughts of surrender. He couldn't let go just yet. Not until he had figured out how to get Emma to safety.

That's a laugh, he thought. *The horse is dead. You're as good as dead. And when you're gone, she'll be better off dead.*

He felt hot tears of rage form at the corners of his eyes. She was only a child, barely twelve, but that wouldn't mean anything to Jerry and his friends. Mac knew what they had in store for her. She would get the same treatment her mother had. The only safety for Emma was with the one round left in his revolver.

Oh, dear Jesus, he thought, *I'm not sure I can do that.*

But what were the alternatives? They were going to be found, of that there was no doubt. Jerry was riding with Armando Chama, and that weasel could track a tadpole through a stream. Mac had managed to turn them back with that last blaze of gunfire, but he knew they wouldn't stay behind for long. At least he had managed to kill Stilly and Jarvis and Earl Harvey. He could still see the look of amazement on Earl's face when the son of a bitch knew he was done for. It was a good memory, and Mac hoped the Lord would forgive him for relishing it.

Outside the cave, there was a gentle thump of approaching hoofbeats, and Mac's pulse began to race. With a slight gasp, he drew his hand away from his wound and slipped the gun from its holster.

The hoofbeats stopped. For a moment there was silence. Mac thought he could hear muffled voices, but he couldn't be sure. Then he heard the crunch and jingle of spur-laden boot heels walking through the undergrowth, coming closer.

Mac pulled back the hammer on the gun. The click seemed to echo off the stones. Emma held him so tightly that he feared she would force the air from his lungs.

God, forgive me, he thought, and he pointed the barrel at her head. Her eyes were closed. She would never know. Never know…

No, he thought. *I can't. I won't.*

Mac snarled and turned the gun to the cave entrance. His last bullet would be for the first murdering bastard who stepped inside. And after that, he still had his knife, and his hands, and his teeth.

The boots stopped moving. Judging from the sound of their approach, Mac thought that the man was standing just to the right of the cave entrance. The gun began to feel heavy in his hand. He watched in dismay as the barrel began to tremble.

"I know that you're in there," someone said. "I know that you've been hurt. I can help you, if you'll let me."

It was a man's voice, deep and unfamiliar. Mac blinked. He knew Jerry's crew, felt certain he'd recognize if it was one of them.

"The choice is yours, my friend," said the voice. "Can we have a talk, or should I just ride on?"

Emma raised her head and Mac looked down into her wide and terrified eyes. "Stay calm, Sugar," he said softly. "I think we might have some hope after all." He squinted at the cave opening and took a ragged breath. "Hey, hombre," he said, and he was pleased that his voice still carried some strength. "Come on in and sit a spell, if you want. There's room for you. Just make sure you move slow and easy. I'm feeling pretty shaky, and my gun's got a hair trigger."

He heard a dry laugh, and somehow he found it chilling and reassuring all at once. "Don't worry," the man said. "An innocent man has nothing to fear from me."

And then the sunlight disappeared as a shadow filled the entrance to the cave.

Blue Hawk and his companion had been tracking the Sheldon Gang through Wyoming Territory for a little over a week. The weather had been dry, and the sign had been easy to spot. Happy Dan Sheldon was almost as good at running as he was at killing, but he wasn't good enough to hide a trail from Blue Hawk.

In the waning light of the ninth day, Blue Hawk came upon something unexpected. He stopped his horse and glanced at his companion. "Look there," he whispered to the man.

The man nodded. "I see it," he said. "It looks fresh."

Blue Hawk silently dismounted and knelt beside the drops of blood. "Less than an hour," he said. He examined the ground for a moment. "There were two on foot," he said, "a man and a child. One of them – the man, I think – tried to cover the tracks but…"

Blue Hawk stood up. He gazed thoughtfully at the rocky, rising slope that flanked the trail. His eyes fell on the dark aperture, and he smiled grimly. He pointed at it and turned to his companion. "They are there, Señor," he said. "I am certain of it."

The other man stepped down from his horse and began to walk deliberately toward the cave. He made no effort at stealth, and Blue Hawk knew that he wanted his approach to be heard. When he reached the entrance, the man stood to one side and spoke in what Blue Hawk thought of as his Running Water Voice, the one he always affected when he was trying to calm and comfort the frightened or the wounded. Blue Hawk often wondered how one man could have so many voices, each so different and so disturbingly effective.

There was a moment of stillness, and then Blue Hawk nodded as he heard a muffled invitation issue from the darkness, and he watched Señor step inside. The Running Water Voice had done its work, as he had known that it would.

Mac squinted up at the silhouette that stood before him, the black shape of a tall man in a broad-brimmed hat. He blinked a few times, then gasped and very nearly pulled the trigger. The man standing before him – the man Mac had dared to hope would be a savior – was wearing a mask. His ice-blue eyes, catching light from God only knew where, gleamed in the shadows beneath his hat.

"An outlaw," Mac rasped. "You'd better keep your distance, mister. I meant what I said about this gun."

"I believe you," the dark man said, calm and even. "And you should believe me when I tell you that I am not an outlaw."

"Then why do you have a mask over your face?"

"This mask *is* my face. I only take it off when I'm in disguise."

"Do you have any idea how crazy you sound?"

The man laughed softly, and again Mac felt oddly reassured by the sound. There was little mirth in it, but no malice either.

"If I took off my gun belt, would that make you feel better?"

Mac nodded. "I think it would."

The dark man slowly removed his belt. After he had done this, he sat cross-legged in front of Mac, laying the guns on the ground beside him. "We can sit in here and chat, if you like," the man said. "But I think you and this child should come out into the light with me. I can see that you've been seriously injured. I have a friend with me who can help you."

"I'm beyond help," Mac said. "I've got a slug in me that's killing me by inches."

"There may still be time…"

Mac shook his head. "Those inches," he said, "they've been building up a while. They've turned into feet. I don't have much distance left to go."

"What about this girl?"

Mac looked down at Emma. She had not uttered a word since he had pulled her onto his horse and carried her away from the death of her parents. She merely clutched at him, whimpering.

"She's not hurt physically," Mac said. "I can't say about her mind. She's seen Hell today. She won't get over it soon. Maybe not ever."

"What happened?"

Mac told him. He tried to keep it short. He was having trouble breathing, and it would have been a hard thing to speak of, even if he hadn't been bleeding to death.

He told him how he had been staying with his son's family, helping them with their small ranch. He told him how he had been heading back from mending fence when, behind the rise, he saw a plume of oily black smoke rising into the air. It wasn't enough to be the house or the barn, but it frightened him and he spurred the old mare to run faster than she should.

When he topped the small hill and had a clear view of his family's home, the first thing he saw was…

The first thing…

Oh, God…

There were ten of them. It was too far away to see them clearly, but he recognized the white Arabian that belonged to Jerry Fenris. There was another familiar animal, a chestnut gelding with a white blaze. It belonged to the sheriff, Tom Henry.

The men were standing in a loose huddle, their attention absorbed by something on the ground.

What the hell are they doing? What's burning?

The smoke was rising from something that looked like a large bundle of rags that lay about twenty yards away from where Jerry's gang was congregated.

Mac raced forward, and after a few seconds the smell hit him; a greasy, cloying stench like burning meat. Then he could hear the laughter, covering barely audible cries.

Mac drew his gun, and pushed the mare harder.

A few seconds that felt like hours passed. One of them turned around and pointed at Mac. It was Pete Stilly. He yelled something and reached for his revolver. Mac didn't hesitate. He fired, and Pete dropped like a stone. Later, Mac would think back on it and realize it was the single best shot he had ever fired.

Then he was among them. They were shouting and cursing and Mac was surprised he wasn't being filled with lead. Then he realized that most of them didn't have their guns on, or even their pants. They were standing around in their long-johns. It would have been almost comical except...

Someone screamed his name. It was his daughter-in-law, Laura. He hadn't seen her at first because she had been on the ground. They had been holding her on the ground. They had been...

Her wrists were pinned by another one Mac knew, a fat cowhand named Jarvis. The man was gawking up at Mac, as if confused as to why the fun was being interrupted. Mac fired at him, but the horse turned at the last moment and the shot went wild.

By now some of the others had gotten to their guns and bullets were whizzing past Mac's head. Mac jumped off the horse, tried to use the poor thing as a shield, started running with the animal toward Laura.

Where was his son? Where was Ned?

Laura was kicking, screaming. The idiot Jarvis was still holding her. She managed to twist away and rose up, clawing madly at his eyes.

Mac felt something thump into his side, and he went numb from his shoulder to his knee. He almost fell, but his grip on the horse's bridle kept him up. He could hear and feel the bullets striking the old mare. She twisted and brayed from the pain, but she stayed on her feet and followed where he led.

Laura turned to him, pointed over his shoulder, screamed something. What?

Emma!

Laura's forehead blew apart. She collapsed and Mac saw Jarvis, still kneeling on the ground, with a smoking gun in his hand. The fat man stared, open-mouthed, at Laura's body. He hadn't seemed to realize that a gun would actually do that. Mac added to his object lesson by shooting him in the chest.

Mac heard his grandaughter cry out for him. He chanced a look over the mare's back and saw her. Her neck was in the crook of Earl Harvey's beefy arm. She bit him. Earl shoved her away, screaming. He raised his gun and…

No! Not like Laura!

Mac pulled the trigger and made a good memory.

Emma had almost reached him. He leapt onto the mare like a man twenty years his junior, grabbed the girl up and dug in his heels to make the old horse run, run, run…

The horse ran by the smoking pile of rags.

No. Not rags.

Mac was past the tree line before he stopped screaming his son's name.

Mac stopped talking. It was getting very hard to breathe.

"How far behind you are they?" the masked man asked.

"I don't know," Mac said softly. "I sent the horse away to make a false trail, but it couldn't have got far, poor thing. I hope there's a heaven for horses."

"I think there is."

Mac nodded. "It might throw them off, but not for long. Armando's too good…"

"Armando Chama?"

"That's the one. You know him?"

"We've met. I thought he was dead, actually."

"Pity you weren't right. Listen, I can't hold out much longer. I ain't never died before, but I can still recognize the feeling. I got no reason to trust you, but I don't see as how I've got much choice. My grand-daughter…"

"I will protect her."

"Well, that's…that's what I needed to hear…Oh God…please be the good man that I think you are…please…"

"She will be safe. You have my word."

Mac tried to respond, to tell the man that he believed him, but couldn't. He used the last of his strength to pull Emma just a little bit closer, and then he was gone.

"This is a terrible thing," Blue Hawk said. "These men, they must be punished."

Señor nodded his agreement, but said nothing. His eyes were focused on some point in the middle distance.

"Do you think they will be here soon?" Blue Hawk asked.

"By nightfall, I think, or shortly thereafter."

"What shall we do?"

Señor turned his gaze to Blue Hawk. "We have to forget about Happy Dan," he said. "We've got a new set of priorities." He gestured to the young girl. She sat on the hillside, head down, her arms around her knees. "We're taking her to San Francisco," Señor continued. "Our friend at the Carlton Hotel can help her –"

"Stop," said the girl.

Señor fell silent. Both he and Blue Hawk looked at the child. "Stop what?" Señor asked in a mild tone.

"Stop talking about me like I wasn't here." The girl lifted her head and met their eyes. She took a shuddering breath. "I know you want to help, and I'm grateful. I really am. But I don't want to run away. I want to fight. I want to...I want to kill those men."

"I am sorry," Señor said. "I understand your feelings, more than you can know, but –"

"You're not listening, Mister," the girl interrupted again, and Blue Hawk was amazed at the steel in her voice. "I'm not going to San Francisco or anywhere else. If you try to make me go, I'll fight you. If tie me up, I'll chew through the ropes. I'm gonna find a gun and I'm gonna kill them fellas. I'll kill them if it's the last thing I do."

Blue Hawk cast an apprehensive glance at the descending sun, then looked at Señor.

"All right," the Masked Rider said to the child. "We will take them apart. Every last one of them."

The girl's eyes widened, as did Blue Hawk's. Señor had spoken in his voice of Burning Blood. It was a quiet voice, but shot through with the rage that Blue Hawk knew boiled like a river of lava inside his friend.

Señor stepped over to the girl and helped her to her feet. "You can help," he said, "but only on my terms. I made a promise to your grandfather and I intend to keep it. You will need to ride with my friend Blue Hawk and do exactly as he says, without question and without hesitation. Will you agree to that?"

The girl looked at Blue Hawk. For a moment she hesitated, then gave a firm nod.

"Very well," Señor said. He turned to Blue Hawk. "I have an idea," he said. "It is very risky and will require a lot of improvisation, but I believe I can make it work."

"I know that you will," Blue Hawk said. "What would you have me do?"

The Masked Rider spoke, and Blue Hawk listened.

Sheriff Tom Henry looked around at the six murderers who rode with him, and told himself that he was not one of them. He had, after all, not laid a finger on the Taylor woman, nor had he assisted in the immolation of her husband. In fact, he had not gone to the small ranch with the intention of hurting anyone.

We're going to put a scare into 'em, Jerry Fenris had said. *If you're with us, it'll take the wind out of their sails completely. They'll know they've got no one to turn to. They'll sell out and go, like they should have done in the first place.*

Tom felt his stomach lurch. They had put a scare into them, all right.

I should have been paying more attention, Tom thought. *It was right there on his face the whole time, all tensed up with the crazy dancing behind his eyes.*

Tom shook his head. All he had seen was some easy money and a chance to curry favor with Jerry's rich old man. Everyone knew that Wayne Fenris despised the Taylors on general principle, as he would anybody who had the nerve to own land he considered his by divine right, if not by the laws of the United States.

So Tom had saddled up to go do a little harmless bullying, and about ten seconds after they trotted into Ned Taylor's yard everything went straight to Hell. *Let's do it boys*, was all Jerry said, and it was as if the door had opened on a cage of rabid dogs.

"What is that?" someone said, snapping Tom out of his reverie. The thick Spanish accent marked the speaker as Chama, the tracker. Not that he was doing a bang-up job of tracking, as far as Tom was concerned. The man hadn't figured out they were following a riderless horse until they had rode up on the mare's carcass, and by the time they picked up Mac's trail they had burned more daylight than they could afford to lose. They were going to have to wrap this thing up soon, before it got so messy that even a sheriff's authority couldn't contain it.

"What are you talking about?" Jerry asked Chama. ""What do you see?"

Chama pointed at the ground. The other men rode up to get a closer look. Tom joined them, and felt the hairs stand up on the back of his neck.

They were looking at a crude drawing in the dirt. Seven stick men on seven stick horses rode with wolfish grins on their little round faces. Behind them was a pair of crude but gruesome renderings of dead people; X marks for their eyes, mouths drawn as crooked lines of pain. A curl of what might have been smoke had been doodled over one of them.

One of the men, Gant, gave a nervous laugh. "You reckon the girl did that?" he asked.

"Don't know and don't care," Jerry said. "Let's get moving. It's going to be dark soon."

There was a general murmur of assent, and they moved forward. Tom could hear Little Frank whispering something to Jerry about the girl. He couldn't quite make out the words, but he didn't really need to. He was under no illusions about what some of these boys had in mind for Emma Taylor. Not all of them had been able to get their turn with Mama.

Tom clenched his teeth. He had reconciled himself to the necessity of the girl's death, but there was no reason she couldn't go quick. There was no need for any of that...other. Tom would see to it.

Chama suddenly pulled up short, cursing in Spanish.

"What is it now?" Jerry snapped.

Chama pointed at the ground, and the men gathered to take a look. Again there were seven stick men. Their teeth were showing, but not in grins. Each of the little men was hanging from gallows. Their arms and legs were twisted at weird angles, and their eyes were big round O's of fear. One of them had a star drawn on his chest.

This time, no one laughed.

Jerry turned to his men and opened his mouth to say something, but he was cut short by a mournful cry that came from somewhere ahead of them. All of the men looked down the trail, although there was nothing to see but gathering shadows.

"That sounded like..." Little Frank began, but he was silenced by a gesture from Jerry. A moment later, they heard the cry again. This time, they were able to make out words. *"Help me,"* the voice was saying.

"That's her," Jerry said. "Let's get a move on!"

"Wait," Tom said.

"Wait?" Jerry said. "Wait for what?"

"Something's wrong here, Jerry. My gut's telling me that—"

"Damn your gut! We don't have time for this!" With that he turned and spurred his horse into a gallop. Little Frank paused to smirk at Tom before following on Jerry's heels along with the other men. Tom, gritting his teeth, wavered for a moment before pushing his horse to catch up.

It wasn't long before the sun had completely disappeared, and they were continuing to rush headlong into a dim blue world of wilderness and night. Jerry, clearly frustrated, held up his hand and slowed his mount to a walk, then to a complete stop.

"What is it?" Chama asked him.

"I don't know." Jerry said. "I just…I need a second to think." He rubbed his temples. "My head is starting to hurt. It's going to be a bad one, damn it. Why does this always have to happen when—"

"Help me."

There a moment of dead silence.

"I don't get it," Gant said. He was whispering, but his voice seemed very loud to Tom. "She sounds just as far away as she did a few minutes ago. How can that be?"

No one answered him. Tom looked around nervously, trying to take in as much of their surroundings as possible. *A hill on one side and trees on the other*, he thought, *and nothing to see by except for moonlight. Looks like there's a bend in the trail ahead of us. Is she up there? Is someone else? We're sitting ducks for…*

For what? For a little girl and a dying old man? What was he so afraid of?

He thought of the star on the stick man's chest.

"I'm afraid of getting what I deserve," he whispered to himself.

"What's that?" Jerry said. "What did you just say?"

"I said we're getting to a curve," Tom replied, pointing. "Up there. I think we should take it slow."

"I think we should go back," someone said.

"Who said that?" Jerry shouted. "Creed? Vance? Who's the coward that wants to hang because they're afraid of the dark?"

"Take it easy, Boss," Little Frank said. "You're gonna make your headache worse."

"Help me."

The voice was closer now. Just around the bend, in fact.

Jerry's teeth gleamed in the moonlight. "Well, boys," he said. "You heard that, right? Let's go help her."

He turned his horse and, just as he began to lead them forward, they heard something, a sizzling sound. There was a sudden flash of light in the darkness, which quickly dimmed into a flickering red radiance that glowed behind the bend in the trail.

That was gunpowder, Tom thought. *Someone just started a fire. Big one, too.*

"Maybe Tom's right," Little Frank said. "Maybe we should go slow."

Jerry's only response was a sneer, but he went slow.

There was a man standing in front of the fire. His back was to them, and though he had surely heard the approach of the horses, he did not in any way acknowledge their presence. He was tall and lean and dressed in dark clothes, his head crowned by a black Stetson. He wore two guns, slung low and butt-forward.

Tom exchanged a glance with Little Frank, and it was one of the very few times they were ever instantly and completely in accord. They both slowly drew their guns.

For his part, Jerry seemed more amused than concerned. He looked over his shoulder at Tom and smiled. He turned back to man before the fire and said, "Evening, Mister."

"Hello, Jerome," the man replied.

Tom felt a hand of ice wrap around his heart.

"You know my name?" Jerry asked.

"I do," the dark man said.

Jerry looked back at Tom. He wasn't smiling anymore. *Who?* he silently mouthed, cocking a thumb at the stranger. Tom shrugged. Jerry shook his head, giving that disgusted I'm-surrounded-by-idiots look that anyone who knew him was familiar with. "It seems you've got me at a disadvantage, Mister," he said. "Can I ask who I'm talking to?"

"I'm the Angel of Death," the man said.

At any other time, it would have been laughable. Tom certainly would have laughed, a long and loud guffaw. *Sure you are,* he would have said, and he would have walked up and punched the "angel" right in the face. Tom

"I am the Angel of Death."

looked at the other men. Maybe it's what they would have done, too. At any other time.

Tom's eye fell on Chama, and he was startled by the expression of stark terror on the tracker's face. "*Yo te conozco,*" the Mexican whispered.

The dark man slowly turned. "And I know you, Armando Chama," he said. It was hard to discern his features, but Tom could see that he was wearing a mask, and that he was smiling. "It's been a long time, *mi amigo.* I guess the Apaches didn't take care of you after all. Don't worry. I'll correct their mistake."

"No," Chama gasped, and he began clutching at his chest. "*Dios!*" he cried. "*Oh, Dios! Oh, Dios!*" His mouth worked frantically, like a fish out of water, and then he fell from his horse. He writhed on the ground for a few brief seconds, and was still.

For a moment, Tom and the others just gawked at him. Then, Little Frank dismounted and checked the man's pulse. Wide-eyed, he looked up at Jerry and shook his head.

The dark man cocked his head. "I can honestly say I didn't expect that," he said.

"Okay," Jerry said, "I think I've had enough of this bullshit." He pulled his gun and pointed at the man's head. "I'm going to ask you one more time. Who the hell are you?"

"Armando knew me as the Masked Rider," the man said. "But I've already told you my real name."

"Cute," Jerry said. "Well, let's see if Death can die."

"If you do that, you'll never find the old man and the little girl."

They all seemed to freeze in tableau, and the only sound was the breathing of the horses and the crackle and hiss of the fire.

"What do you know about them?" Jerry asked.

"Everything," said the Masked Rider.

"Where are they?"

"That's going to cost you, Jerome."

"How much?"

"Why don't you come over here and we'll discuss it."

Jerry dismounted.

"Hold on, Boss," Little Frank whispered. "You're not thinking straight. You know how you get when your head's hurting…"

Jerry ignored him and, gun hand extended, marched up to the Masked Rider. He stopped a few feet in front of him, the barrel of the gun almost touching the space between the dark man's eyes.

Tom shifted uneasily in his saddle. Jerry had effectively blocked the field of fire for all of his men, and that wasn't even the worst of it. The damned fool was acting like he was facing some quaking homesteader who was about to start begging for mercy. Was he completely blind?

Maybe he was, but Tom certainly was not, and he saw something that made him shudder. It was a small thing, really, and it was a miracle that he had caught it. Nonetheless, he did catch it, and he recognized it immediately.

The dark man…*relaxed*. What little tension had been inside of him simply dissolved. Tom saw it in the set of the man's shoulders, in the turn of his head, in the way he stood. It was the subtle transformation that occurs in a man when he knows that the crisis has passed, and he is now in complete control.

"Jerry," Tom said, low and cautious, "I think that you should—"

The thought was never completed. It was interrupted by a sudden flash of movement – if shadows can be said to flash – from the Masked Rider. For a single, strange moment, the two men appeared to be dancing together before the fire, and then Jerry was facing his men, his neck encircled in the Rider's left arm. Jerry's gun, which had been deftly plucked from his hand, was now firmly pointed at his temple.

How did he do that? Tom marveled. Jerry appeared to be wondering the same thing. It had happened so quickly that he had not even had time to cry out. He opened his mouth to speak, and nothing emerged but a feeble squeak of protest. He twisted and shuffled, bug-eyed and helpless in the dark man's iron grip.

"You're choking him!" Little Frank said.

"Yes, I am," the Rider replied. "His headache's going to get a lot worse, I'm afraid. Maybe I should do something to take his mind off of it." Then he lowered the gun and shot out Jerry's right knee.

Jerry tried to scream, but he didn't have the air.

The horses shifted nervously, but they were accustomed to gunfire and took it in stride. The same could not be said for Jerry's men.

"Stop!" Little Frank shrieked. "Don't do that! Don't do anything like that again!"

"You should calm down, Franklin," the Rider said. "You don't want to end up like Armando. Why don't you pretend I'm threatening a helpless little girl? Maybe then you'll feel better."

Maybe it did at that, because Frank visibly regained his nerve. He even holstered his revolver. Tom was impressed in spite of himself, but he couldn't understand why the little man would go into near hysterics over such a thing in the first place. He and Jerry were obviously closer than anyone realized.

"Listen," Frank said, "I don't know who you are, or how you're tied up in all this, but I'll tell you something. The only way you're gonna get out of this alive is if you let him go right now. You savvy?"

"I do," said the Rider, "but I disagree. If I were to let go of this maggot, that would be your cue to open up on me with everything you've got, now wouldn't it?"

"I'd have to say you're right about that, Mister," Tom said. He kept a friendly, casual tone, as if he were agreeing that yes, it did look like rain. He moved his horse forward, gently nudging Frank aside. "Now, I can speak for everyone here when I say that we'd like to see Jerry to live at least until the next payday. So why don't you just tell us what you want, and maybe we can come to an understanding."

"Okay," said the Rider. "I'd like you to go find some rope and hang yourselves."

"You don't want much, do you?" Tom said.

Jerry's eyes fluttered, and he went limp in the Rider's arm. The dark man continued to hold him without any apparent effort, but he slightly loosened his grip. Tom could tell because he heard a wheeze as Jerry resumed breathing.

"You got an alternative suggestion?" Tom asked.

"Yes," said the Rider. "Everyone leaves at a gallop but you. Ten minutes later, I let you take Jerry home to Daddy."

"And then?"

The Rider shrugged. "Do what you like. It really doesn't matter. You're dead men. All of you."

"You don't lack for confidence, I'll give you that," Tom said. He looked over his shoulder. "You heard the man, boys. Get out of here. Vance, you can lead Armando's horse and pick up the ones we left at the Taylor place. Creed, you take Jerry's. Gant, go to town and get Doc Purvis."

"Purvis?" Gant said. "What for?"

"What the hell do you think?" Tom shouted, pointing at Jerry.

"What am I supposed to tell him?"

"Just tell him Jerry got shot and if he needs to know more he can ask me later. I'll think of something."

"What about Armando?" Vance asked.

"Leave him," Tom said. "He'll only slow you down."

"Don't seem right," Vance said.

"Well, if it bothers you so damned much, load him up! And on your way back, make sure you give Ned Taylor and his wife a Christian burial, too!"

Vance grabbed the reins of Armando's stallion and turned to go.

"Wait a minute!" Little Frank said. "Tom, have you gone completely crazy? You're going to trust this bastard? What the hell's wrong with you?"

"Frank," Tom said, "Jerry is bleeding to death right now. If we keep wasting time, I won't be able to bring him home alive. If that happens, what do you think his father will do?"

Frank muttered a stream of curses, but he jumped on his horse without any further protest. "Let's go!" he shouted to the others, and, as they had been commanded, they started down the trail at a gallop.

Tom did not watch them go. He continued to stare at the dark man as the hoofbeats receded into the distance.

At length, the Masked Rider spoke. "Put away your gun and dismount," he said. "I will allow you to dress his wound."

Tom obeyed. As he approached, the Rider dropped Jerry to the ground and stepped away. To Tom's complete astonishment, the man opened Jerry's gun, emptied it, and tossed it into the woods.

"I can't believe you just did that," Tom said.

"Why? I have guns of my own."

"Yeah, but..."

"But I've thrown away my advantage? I suppose you're right. Here I am, empty-handed. This is your chance, Thomas. Are you going to make a move?"

"Are you really so sure I couldn't take you?"

The Rider said nothing.

Tom ground his teeth. The man's casual contempt was humiliating. He shook his head and applied himself to the task of putting a tourniquet above Jerry's knee. It was an extreme measure – Jerry would probably lose his leg – but Tom just didn't know what else to do. He certainly wasn't going to ask the Rider for help.

Jerry gasped, and Tom winced as he realized the young man was regaining consciousness. "Be quiet and don't move," he said. "You're in bad shape and just about anything you do is apt to make it worse."

"What?" Jerry moaned. "What the...Oh, Jesus, my leg..."

"Dammit Jerry, I said to shut up!"

Jerry nodded and choked off his cries, biting his lips until the blood came.

Tom looked up at the Rider. "You didn't have to do that, you know. Shoot him like that."

"He didn't have to force a child to watch her own mother be gang raped," the Rider said.

Tom was unable to stop himself. "I didn't know that was going to happen," he said. "I didn't know and I wasn't part of it."

"Oh, I see," said the Rider. "You just watched."

Tom didn't answer. He tied off the tourniquet and sat back on his heels. Jerry was pale and sweating, his eyes closed tight as he silently wept. An image of the Taylor woman flashed into Tom's mind, the way her face had looked when they put the torch to her husband...

"It happened so fast," Tom said. "They were just...They went blood-crazy. I've seen it before. I couldn't have stopped them if I'd tried."

The Rider said nothing.

Tom did not dare to look at the man. He felt as if he were under the shadow of the gallows.

Jerry opened his eyes. "Tom," he said, his voice a barely audible croak.

Tom leaned down, and Jerry spit in his face.

"Coward," Jerry said. "You weren't a part of it, huh? You make me want to puke."

Tom pulled a handkerchief out of his pocket and wiped the bloody spittle from his face and eyes. He stood up and turned to the Rider. "I think the ten minutes are about up," he said.

"Just about," said the Rider.

"You know we're going to come after you, right?"

"I'm counting on it."

Tom nodded. "Mac's already dead, isn't he?"

"He is."

"The girl..."

"Is safe, and she's going to stay that way."

Tom looked up at the moon. It was full and red; a hunter's moon. He turned back and looked into the dark man's cold, cold eyes. "Why are you doing this?" he asked.

"Why are *you*?" the Rider said.

Tom shook his head. "I can't back out now. I'm in too deep. There's nothing else for me but to see it through to the end."

"The same is true for me," the Rider replied. "It has been for as long as I can remember."

"Then I reckon we understand each other," Tom said. He grabbed Jerry, none too gently, and lifted him onto the back of his horse. As they turned to go, Jerry lifted a shaking hand and pointed at the Masked Rider. "I'll see you again, you son of a bitch," he said.

"You certainly will, boy," the Rider said, "and that will be the day I bear you off to Hell."

Wayne Fenris was a big man, a solid six-foot-three of muscle and bone. The entire house seemed to shake as he paced to and fro in his study, listening with an ever-deepening frown to Tom's account of the evening's activities. He did not interrupt, but he would occasionally pause to glower at Tom in shock or rage, then resume his thundering march back and forth, back and forth.

When Tom finally ran out of words, the elder Fenris turned his back and leaned heavily on his desk, as if the weight of the world, or at least several dead bodies, was pressing down on him. "Did Jerome…did he violate the woman?" he asked.

"He took the first turn," Tom said.

"Who killed Ned Taylor?"

"It was Jerry's idea to burn him, but the others did most of the work."

Wayne sighed heavily. "This masked man, do you have any idea who he is? Where he came from?"

"None whatsoever. The only thing I can say for sure is that he must have had a good little parley with Mac. He knew what had happened. He knew our names."

Wayne turned and glared at Tom. "How could you let all this happen?"

"How could I…? What the hell are you talking about? None of this would have happened in the first place if you weren't so damn-all eager for the Taylors to be gone!"

"That's beside the point! I only told Jerome that he and the boys should rough them up a little. I never said a thing about killing anyone."

"Well, I guess Jerry had his own ideas."

"None of this is his fault!" Wayne bellowed.

Tom's jaw dropped. "Good God, Wayne! How can you say that? He was the ramrod for the whole thing!"

"He can't help himself," Wayne sputtered. "He's always had problems controlling himself. I don't know why. It has something to do with those headaches. You know that, Tom. You know that and by God you should have stepped in and done something! As far as I'm concerned, you are completely responsible for this fiasco!"

Tom rose from his chair. "Now you listen to me," he said. "I have had just about enough of everybody pointing their fingers at me, judging me, spitting in my face…"

"What? What is that supposed to mean, spitting…?"

"Never mind. What matters now is figuring out how we're going to get out of this mess. If you've got any big ideas, I'd love to hear 'em."

Wayne chewed his lower lip. He looked like a little kid reaching for a lie to cover his truancy. A minute or so went by, and Tom grew increasingly restive. He thought about just walking out. Why not? He could just get on his horse and head north, go straight to Canada. If he left right now, right this very instant, he could get enough of a head start to…

Someone was shouting in the next room.

"What's going on out there?" Wayne snapped.

The door to the study flew open and Little Frank almost fell in ahead of Tom's young deputy, Joe Keefer. "Sheriff!" Joe shouted. "Thank God! Thank God I've found you! Something terrible has happened! Something awful!"

Yes, it has, Tom thought.

Someone had been to the Taylor place.

Someone had seen the bodies.

Someone had come to town and told Joe all about it.

All of this came spilling out of Joe in a nearly incomprehensible deluge of babbling. As Tom well knew, the boy had nursed an innocent crush on the Taylor woman for months, and the thought of her dead and defiled was obviously ripping him apart.

"We've got to get up there, Sheriff…We've got to…My God, how could anyone…She was so beautiful…"

"Easy, there, Joe," Tom said. He noticed Little Frank's hand straying to his gun and felt a stab of panic. Somehow he had to take control of this thing. He slowly eased himself between Frank and Joe. "Calm down, son. Tell me, the fella who stumbled on to all this, did you bring him with you?"

"He's right outside, Sheriff. I know he's telling the truth, 'cause he described Missus Taylor…he saw…"

"We know all about it, Joe," Wayne Fenris said. He was very somber, very grave.

Joe Keefer suddenly became very still. He looked up at Fenris, then at Tom. "You do?" he said.

"Yes," Tom said, after the briefest of pauses. "I'll let Mr. Fenris tell you." He looked at Wayne. "Tell him, sir. I think it would be better coming from you."

"Of course, Tom, of course," Wayne said. He leaned back on his desk and crossed his arms. "Joe, earlier today I sent my son and some of his men up to Ned Taylor's to discuss a business proposition. I asked Sheriff Henry here to tag along, as a witness you understand. Everyone knows Ned and I don't – didn't – get along. On the way there, they ran into Mac Taylor, and he joined up with them.

"Anyway, when the boys arrived, they stumbled onto a terrible scene. The Taylor ranch was being attacked by a band of outlaws. Ten men at least. They had already killed Ned and I suppose you know what they were doing with his wife.

"Naturally, my men tried to stop them. There was a gunfight. Pete Stilly, Bo Jarvis, and Earl Harvey were killed. Mrs. Taylor was also killed in the crossfire. One of the outlaws snatched up the Taylor child—"

"Emma," Joe said. "Her name is Emma."

"Yes, Emma, of course. One of the outlaws snatched her up and they fled. My men gave chase. They lost them in the foothills, but then they caught up with the bastards when they tried to make camp. They traded shots again, and my son was wounded in the leg. Mac Taylor told Tom and the boys to get him home, and then he – uh, Mac that is – and Armando Chama went on after the outlaws."

Wayne looked at Tom. "I think that's everything, isn't it Sheriff?"

"Oh, yeah," Tom replied. "You've covered all the facts."

"Yes," Wayne said. He turned his eyes back to Joe. "As you can see," he said, "we're going to have to get a posse on the trail of these killers at first light. We'll follow them right to gates of Hell if we have to. I just pray nothing happens to the little…to Emma. We have to be very careful. The last thing we want to happen is for her to be shot in the crossfire by the people who are trying to save her."

"The very last thing," Tom affirmed.

Joe's eyes were locked with Tom's. *He knows something isn't right*, Tom thought. *He knows but he can't put his finger on it.* Tom began to silently plead with Joe to just nod, or cry, or scream, or do pretty much anything but ask questions. *Don't push it, boy*, he thought. *Don't make me choose between you and my own neck.*

"I don't understand why..." Joe said, and maybe it would have been his epitaph if he had completed the thought, but he was cut off by someone entering the study.

"I didn't mean to eavesdrop," the intruder said, "but I heard what you said, and it fits right in with what I saw."

Tom regarded this interloper with something not unlike gratitude. He was a rangy, raw-boned cowboy, no different from any of the other drifters who passed through every month or so. He carried his roll-brimmed hat like a humble supplicant approaching royalty. He was older than Joe, but he had same sort of open, honest countenance that the deputy always wore. He would have been the very picture of innocence if it weren't for the two low-slung six-guns that hung about his waist.

"And who might you be?" Tom asked.

"Name's Wade Morgan," the cowboy said, "I found the bodies, and I think I know who killed them folks."

Tom and Wayne spoke in unison: "You do?" There was an awkward pause as they glanced at one another in mutual embarrassment.

"Uh, yeah," Morgan said. "I'm pretty sure this is the work of the Sheldon Gang."

"The Sheldon Gang," Wayne said, as if this meant something to him. He looked at Tom, and said it again: "The Sheldon Gang."

An image from a wanted poster back at the office flashed into Tom's mind, a scowling face with sleepy eyes and a drooping moustache. "Happy Dan Sheldon," Tom said, and he felt pleased with himself for recalling the name. "I thought he was somewhere in Nebraska."

"He was," Morgan said, "but now he's here. I've been following him for a couple of weeks."

"Why is that?" Tom asked.

Morgan shrugged. "Times are tough," he said, "and Happy Dan's got a price on his head. I'm a cowhand, not a bounty hunter, but I thought maybe I could get lucky..."

"Well, this most fortunate," Wayne said. "Most fortunate, indeed. Now we know who the culprits are, and we can get after them with all due haste! Are you a decent tracker, sir?"

"Better than most," Morgan said.

"Good enough! I understand your pursuit of this man is motivated by profit, and there is nothing wrong with that. Indeed, I applaud it. With that in mind, I have a proposition for you."

"Mr. Fenris," Tom said. "Can I say something here?"

Apparently he couldn't, because Wayne ignored him. "Mr. Morgan, I would like for you to join forces with my men and Sheriff Henry here. If you can assist them in recovering the Taylor child, I will pay you double the reward offered for this criminal. Double! Does that sound like a good offer to you?"

"Real good," Morgan said.

"Excellent." Wayne turned to Tom. "Sheriff, we'll leave at first light. I'd like for you, Joe, and Mr. Morgan to be my guests tonight. I suppose we'll need to—"

"Mr. Fenris," Joe said. "I'm sorry to interrupt, Mr. Fenris, but I need to go back to town for the others."

"What are you talking about?" Tom asked.

"Reverend Hayes and George Brennan, sir. They volunteered to be in the posse."

"The preacher and the undertaker," Tom said. It just kept getting better and better.

"Oh, you might need 'em," Morgan said. "You're going after some of the toughest men you could ask for, hardened killers. The more guns you have, the better off you'll be."

"But *you* were going after them alone," Tom said.

"Well, it's like I said, I thought I might get lucky."

Tom shook his head. "Too many men," he said. "They'll only get in each other's way."

"Oh, nonsense, Tom," Wayne said. "Mr. Morgan's right. Overwhelming force, that's the way to go. Just remember, our first priority is the safety of the child. She must be found, and soon. I assume we can all agree on that?"

Everyone said that they did.

"Very well, then." Wayne said. He gestured at Little Frank, all but forgotten in the far corner where he had been quietly listening. "Frank, please show Mr. Morgan to the guest room."

"With all due respect, sir," Morgan said, "I'd rather head back to town with the deputy. I don't want to impose on your hospitality."

"Suit yourself. We will meet you there just after dawn. Be ready to ride."

"We will be," Joe said, and Morgan nodded.

A moment later, they were gone. Tom collapsed into a chair and sighed.

"I thought that went rather well," Wayne said.

Tom looked at him. "Why the hell do you want to bring along a posse from town?"

"The more the merrier," Wayne said. He poured a glass of brandy from a decanter on his desk. He did not offer any to Tom.

"I'm not sure I'm following your logic," Tom said.

Wayne grinned. It made him look a lot like his son. "Now that we've established that the Masked Rider is part of this…what were their names?

"The Sheldon Gang."

"Ah, yes, Happy Dan, God bless him." Wayne raised his glass in a toast and took a long drink. "Now that we've established that, I'd be happy to have every gun in the territory with us."

"You would?"

"Oh, absolutely! We're going to run that masked man to ground, and when we find him, the lead is going to fly thick and fast. We're going to make sure of it. I'm afraid the little girl won't survive. Who knows? It may even be you who fires the tragic bullet."

Tom heard Little Frank give a muffled laugh.

Tom awoke from a fitful sleep about an hour before sunrise. After he had dressed, he stepped out on to the porch and found Doc Purvis sitting in a rocking chair, sucking on an unlit pipe. "You need a match?" Tom asked him.

"Excuse me?" Purvis said. "Oh, I see. No, no thank you. I didn't even realize it had gone out."

Tom shrugged and rolled himself a cigarette. "How's Jerry?" he asked.

"I'm pretty sure I can save his leg," the doctor said.

"Is that so?" Tom said. "That should earn you a little something extra. I was afraid that I'd done the wrong thing. Putting on the tourniquet, I mean. I guess it was a good move after all, right?"

"You did what you thought you had to do," Purvis said. Tom didn't think that was much of an answer, but he didn't feel inclined to pursue the issue. It wasn't like anyone was going to be showing him much gratitude one way or the other.

"I've given him a significant amount of morphine for the pain," the doctor said.

"How's that working out?"

"As well as can be expected. Morphine is very effective, you know. Very effective."

"The more the merrier."

Tom realized that Purvis had not looked at him a single time during their exchange. He had sat perfectly still in his chair, a whisper-thin shadow speaking in low, quiet tones. Tom was struck by the sudden, bizarre notion that Purvis was dead. The old doctor had sat out here and quietly died in the cool autumn night, and Tom was talking to a ghost. As ridiculous as the thought was, Tom was unable to dismiss it. He walked in front of Purvis and leaned over, looking into his eyes.

"Is something wrong, Sheriff?" Purvis asked.

"Not at all," Tom said. Embarrassed, he turned away and leaned on the porch railing.

"Can I ask something?" Purvis said.

"Sure."

"Can you explain to me exactly what happened at the Taylor place?"

"I thought Wayne had already told you," Tom said. He lit up and took a long drag from the cigarette.

"He wasn't actually there. You were."

"I don't know if I feel like going over it right now."

There was a heavy silence.

"It must have been horrible," the doctor said.

"Yes."

"Jerry has been talking about it."

Tom coughed. "He has?"

"Yes, in his sleep."

"What does he say?"

"It's hard to make out, but it's very strange…very strange…"

Tom slowly turned to face the old man. "Well, Doc, he's been shot and he's pumped full of dope. I'd be surprised if what he was saying *wasn't* strange."

"True enough…True enough…"

"And like you said, I was there. I know what happened. So we don't need to be worried about whatever Jerry Fenris rambles about in his sleep, do we?"

Purvis did not move, did not speak.

"Do we?" Tom repeated.

"I suppose not," the doctor said.

Tom nodded. He turned away and gazed off into the distance. A faint, burnt-orange glow began to appear on the horizon.

"Looks like it's going to be a beautiful day," Tom said.

There was very little talk on the ride to town. Tom was grateful. Purvis had given him all of the conversation he could stand. He felt numb, disconnected from himself. How had all of this happened?

Jerry and his boys had been up to all kinds of no good for months, but it hadn't been a problem. Not for Tom, anyway. Things began to get more serious when Jim Holland's place "accidentally" caught fire. Holland and his wife had barely escaped with their lives. Jim had been so thoroughly cowed by the ordeal that he had immediately sold out and left. A satisfactory conclusion, all told, but it could have gone a lot worse. *Your son's pushing his luck*, Tom had told Wayne Fenris.

Don't you worry about my son, Wayne said. *He does what's necessary, which is more than can be said of you. Just remember who you really work for. That's all you need to do.*

The memory of the conversation filled Tom with a rush of anger. He looked at Wayne, riding beside him on a dark bay stallion.

Wayne noticed. "What's wrong with you?" he asked.

"Nothing. I was just remembering who I work for."

Wayne frowned in puzzlement. He spurred his animal ahead, and stayed there for the rest of the ride.

They arrived in town to an unexpected sight. Parked near the stables behind the hotel were three Murphy wagons. They were absurdly clean, their bonnets gleaming white in the morning sun.

"Who do those belong to?" Wayne asked.

"I don't know," Tom said. "They must have come in late yesterday."

They drew up beside them, and Tom dismounted for a closer look. He could see that they had been modified for rough terrain. They were smaller and lighter than the usual models, with iron reinforced axles.

"Good morning," someone said. "May I be of assistance?"

Tom turned and saw a small, well-dressed man with a neatly trimmed goatee emerge from the shadows of the stables. Around his waist were two revolvers, butt-forward. Tom thought of the masked man and felt his muscles tense. Was it possible that…?

No, it wasn't. This man was too short, for one thing. He wasn't even as tall as Little Frank. He would have to stand on a soapbox to hold Jerry in the crook of his arm.

The man walked up to Tom and extended a hand in greeting. He wore tight leather gloves like some Eastern dandy, but Tom could sense the man's strength as he shook his hand.

"My name is Anton Karlo," the man said. His voice was thick with a strange accent that Tom had never heard before. His tongue seemed to be rolling all around the words, as if he was giving each of them a taste before he let them escape his mouth. "I take it from your badge that you are the constable."

"Sheriff," Tom corrected. "Name's Tom Henry. Do these wagons belong to you?"

The man smiled. "Regrettably, no. They belong to my employer, the Baron Otto Von Engel. I am merely part of his retinue."

"His what?"

Karlo gestured to the wagons. "The Baron is visiting from Deutsch... um...from Germany."

"Germany?" Tom said, utterly baffled. "What is he doing here?"

"He has come here to hunt," Karlo said. "Surely this can come as no surprise to you. The American West is one of the finest hunting grounds in the world."

"Really?" someone said. It was Vance, and he sounded genuinely intrigued. All of the men had drawn closer, their curiosity piqued by this exotic character.

"Oh, yes," Karlo said. "The Wyoming Territory alone can provide a lifetime's worth of sport. The game here is marvelous! Elk, bear, bighorn sheep. The Baron was the envy of all his acquaintances when he announced this expedition."

"Well, give him my regards," Tom said. He mounted his horse and turned to the others. "Okay, boys," he said, "now that we've solved this little mystery, I think we've got some more important business to attend to."

Tom pointed in the general direction of his office, and the others understood. He was falling in behind them, when Karlo called out to him.

"Sheriff," he said. "If you could wait for a moment..."

"Sorry, Mr. Karlo. I'm in the middle of something right now. If the Baron is still in town when I get back, I'll buy you and him both a drink."

"But I think that my employer will be—"

"Good bye, Mr. Karlo. Happy hunting."

⁂

There was an unfamiliar gray roan tethered to the hitching post in front of Tom's office. The question of who it belonged to was settled when Tom saw Morgan waiting for them on the porch. The lanky cowhand was leaning back in a chair, watching them through a haze of cigarette smoke. He touched the brim of his hat in greeting as they approached.

"Where's Deputy Keefer?" Tom asked. He was irked to find Morgan lounging around like he owned the place, and Joe nowhere in sight.

"He went to get the other fellas," Morgan said. "He's been gone a while. I figure he'll be along shortly."

"He'd damn well better be," snarled Wayne Fenris. "I told you idiots that I wanted you ready to ride when we got here."

If it bothered Morgan to be called an idiot, he didn't let it show. "No need to get worked up," he said. "The men who killed them poor folks won't get away. They're all going to pay for what they done. I can promise you that."

Morgan's eyes met with Tom's, and for the briefest of moments he felt a glimmer of…something. *You're tall enough*, Tom thought. *But your voice is all wrong. And God knows you wouldn't have any reason to be here. You'd have to be insane…*

"Sheriff!" someone shouted. "Mr. Fenris!"

Tom recognized Joe's voice, but he didn't turn to see him. He found himself unable to look away from Morgan's ice-blue eyes.

"Something on your mind, Sheriff?" Morgan asked.

"No," said Tom. "I was just thinking that you reminded me of someone, that's all."

Morgan smiled.

"Sheriff," Joe said. He was close now, almost beside Tom. "Sheriff, I've got good news. These people are going to help us."

Tom looked at him. "Yeah, I know. Brennan and the Reverend. You told us all about it. Are they ready to…" Tom trailed off as he noticed the faces of the riders behind Joe. Hayes and Brennan were there, but there were others as well. A florid, barrel-chested man with a bright red beard rode up on a shining black horse. He had the look and manner of a country gentleman bound for a Sunday service. This image of benign gentry was broken only by his hard, gray eyes and the rifle in the leather scabbard on his horse's right side. The man gave Tom a curt nod, which he returned without thinking. "Who are you?" Tom asked.

"You are speaking to the Baron Von Engel," said Anton Karlo, who was riding behind the burly gent. "He cannot speak English, so you should address your questions to me."

"Right," said Tom. "And who's that behind you?"

Karlo made a gesture, and a wan, dark-haired girl rode up. She was about fifteen, maybe sixteen, years old. Her face, though strikingly beautiful, was as pale and expressionless as a porcelain mask. She was dressed in a black riding outfit which appeared to have been custom-made to fit her slender frame. She looked to Tom like a life-sized doll that someone had sat on the back of a pony.

"This is Valentine," Karlo said. "She is my daughter."

Franklin Pettigrew – Little Frank to all and sundry – felt something gnawing inside of him at the sight of the dark-haired girl. It was a familiar feeling, one he had known most of his life, but had never completely understood. Once, late at night, he had described it to Jerry Fenris.

"It's the wolf inside," Jerry had told him.

"I don't follow," Frank said. He had been drinking, but not so much that he couldn't recognize when a statement didn't make sense.

"I know you, Frank," Jerry said. "You're like me. I've got one inside me, too."

Frank laughed. "So we're a couple of werewolves? I like that. Let's go howl at the moon."

"I'm not joking, Frank," Jerry said. "I saw how you were looking at old Harmon's daughter last week when we went in the general store."

"What of it? I like looking at her. She's easy on the eyes."

Jerry shook his head. "There's different ways of looking, Frank. For example, there's the way Jim Holland looks at that bitch he's married to..." Jerry stretched his features into a mask of despairing, henpecked submission. It looked so much like Holland that Frank laughed until he was out of breath. "Show me another one," he said.

"Okay, here's Ned Taylor looking at his cow of a wife." Jerry's eyes went soft with a sort of dreamy detachment. He looked so genuinely lovelorn that Frank stopped laughing. Then Jerry winked at him, shattering the illusion. "I do that pretty good, don't I?"

Frank nodded. "Yeah," he said, "but what about me? You were talking about the way I was looking."

"This is you," Jerry said, and his gaze hardened into something sharp and predatory. His jaw clenched and his nostrils flared and a sneer played at the corner of his mouth.

"Jesus," Frank muttered. "I don't...I didn't think..."

Jerry smiled, but it didn't touch his glittering, hungry eyes. "Relax," he said. "You got nothing to be ashamed of. Not with me, anyway. I look at her that way, too. I look at all of 'em that way."

"I've never seen..."

"Of course you haven't. I hide it better than you. It's not easy though, hiding it. I think it's part of the reason I get these headaches."

"Jerry...Boss... I'm sorry, but you're just confusing me now. Maybe it's cause I'm a little drunk but..."

Jerry reached out and put his hand on Frank's shoulder. "Frank," he said, "what were you thinking when you had that look on your face, when you were staring at Harmon's daughter?"

"C'mon, Jerry, I don't wanna..."

The hand on Frank's shoulder squeezed. It was gentle, reassuring, brotherly. "Tell the truth," Jerry said. "What were you thinking that you would like to do to her?"

Frank told him. It was scary, saying it out loud, but exciting, too. Especially when Jerry just kept smiling, encouraging him to say more, to go into details. Frank obliged him. It was, Frank later reflected, the first time in his life that anyone had seemed interested in what he had to say.

"Well," Jerry said at last, "I think I've heard enough. Let's go."

"Huh? Go where, Boss? It's the middle of the night."

"Out to Harmon's place. I'm pretty sure we can get into the girl's room without waking anybody up."

"Are you serious?"

Jerry grinned, and then Frank saw it. "Boss," he said softly, "your wolf is showing."

Jerry roared with laughter and led his friend into the darkness.

It went just as he said it would. They were able to get the Harmon girl – Frank never did catch her name – out of the house without a sound. Jerry seemed to have some practice at this. They took their time with her, and returned her a couple of hours before dawn. They were sure of her silence. Jerry had told her in excruciating detail what would become of her family if she so much as uttered a word.

For Frank, it was the most incredible experience of his life. Sure, he had thought about such things, but actually *doing* them...Well, once just wasn't enough.

Jerry understood. *Tell me, Frank, what do you think of Ned Taylor's wife?*

Frank told him, and together they made a plan. It was Jerry's idea to involve the other boys. Frank hadn't liked that much, but Jerry was fixed on it. He seemed to like talking them into it. Dragging in Tom Henry had been even more worrisome. *I want him there,* Jerry said to Frank's objections. *I want him up to his neck in it.*

It was all very strange to Frank, but in the end he decided he didn't really care. Jerry had become the best…the only…friend that he had ever had. Frank would go along with anything he said, as long as it gave him another chance to let the wolf run wild.

He had his chance, and watched everything fall to pieces as a result. He had lost Jerry, at least temporarily, and would have to think for himself. And what he was thinking about now was this sweet young thing that – *please oh please let it be true!* – was going to be riding with the posse.

It suddenly occurred to him that his eagerness, his hunger, might be showing on his face. He glanced around to see if anyone was watching him. He was pleased to see that everyone's eyes were fixed on the foreigners and Tom Henry, who was making some noises about not wanting them along.

He almost sighed with relief, and then he saw Morgan.

Morgan was looking right at him.

Can he see? Frank wondered, and the thought filled him with all the terror and rage of a cornered beast. He quickly turned away and focused on Tom, tried to listen to whatever he was jabbering about. It wasn't long, though, before his attention turned again to the girl, her smooth clear skin, the slight curves of her slender body…

He decided he didn't care what Morgan may or may not have seen. It was stupid to even worry about it. Jerry was the only person who could pick up on that sort of thing. No one else cared enough to notice.

I wish you were here, Boss, Frank thought. *I can't wait to tell you all about this one. Maybe I'll even bring her to you, so you can see for yourself.*

Frank smiled, and for just a moment all of the shocks and anxieties of the last twelve hours faded into a red mist of primal anticipation. He felt like howling at the moon.

"No!" Tom said. "I can't believe I'm even having this conversation! Are you completely out of your mind! A teen-age girl in a posse to hunt murderers and…and…"

"Rapists," Morgan volunteered.

Tom shot him a look, and was relieved to see that, judging by Morgan's frown, the man seemed to share his opinion of the whole thing. "Right!" Tom said. "Rapists!"

To Tom's amazement, Karlo seemed completely unmoved. "Your deputy has explained this to us quite thoroughly. We understand the nature of the men we will be hunting."

"Is that so?" Tom said. "Well, thank you, Joe Keefer!"

"I didn't know they were going to bring the girl," Joe said in a weak voice.

"The boy is telling you the truth," Karlo said. "I did not think to mention it to him. Valentine, she is a part of me. I do not go anywhere without her."

"Good," Tom said. "Then you won't go."

There was burst of chatter from the red-haired German. Karlo responded to him, and the Baron rolled his eyes in exasperation. He turned and growled some foreign gibberish at Tom.

"The Baron Von Engel," Karlo said, "wishes to know if you are in charge of this expedition."

Tom said, "Tell him—"

"I am," said Wayne Fenris.

Karlo hesitated. His eyes flicked back and forth between Tom and Wayne.

"With all due respect, *Mr. Fenris*," Tom said, "this is a law enforcement matter, not a cattle drive. I think you would do well to remember that."

"With all due respect, *Sheriff Henry*, you've already had your chance and we've seen how that turned out. Three men dead. Another two unaccounted for. My son fighting for his life even as we speak. I think it would be best if someone else were giving the orders, don't you?"

Tom looked around at the assembled posse. Only Morgan was willing to look him in the eye. "What do you think, drifter?" Tom said to him. "Would you feel more comfortable with Mr. Fenris running the show?"

"That's between you fellas," Morgan said. "I'm just the hired help."

Tom looked at Karlo. "Well," he said, "I guess that goes for me, too. Tell your boss that I'm just the hired help."

Karlo translated. The Baron listened carefully, then reached into a saddlebag. His hand came out with a large pouch which he tossed to Wayne.

"The Baron wishes very much to be included in this hunt," Karlo said. "He is prepared to pay handsomely for the privilege."

Wayne opened the pouch and eyed its contents. "Very handsomely, I see."

"Yes," replied Karlo. "However, the Baron insists that I accompany him, and, as I have stated, I will not be parted from Valentine."

"You're going to stick to that?" Wayne asked. "Even knowing the risks involved?"

"Do not worry," Karlo said. "I will answer for her safety, and I give you my word that she will in no way hinder this expedition."

Wayne thoughtfully hefted the pouch, then dropped it into his saddlebag. "Fine," he said. "Be it on your own head. But understand this, the Baron may be a big dog over in Germany, but on this ride he takes orders me. Got it?"

There was a brief exchange between Karlo and Von Engel.

"The Baron says those terms are acceptable," Karlo said.

"All right, then," Wayne said. "Welcome aboard." He turned to Morgan. "We're going to head for the last spot the outlaws were seen. Do you think you can pick up a trail from there?"

"I think we've got some other business to attend to first," said Reverend Hayes.

"And what might that be?" Wayne asked.

Hayes sidled up beside Wayne until their horses were almost touching. "I believe there are some bodies that need to be given a proper burial," he said softly.

Wayne blinked. "Oh, yes, yes," he said. "It's just...I'm so concerned about this child..."

"Preacher's right," Morgan said. "We can't leave them folks like that, leave 'em for the vultures. Besides, I think you ought to see for yourself what these killers did. You should know the kind of scum you're dealing with."

Tom could see that Wayne did not like the idea. The rancher was in a hurry to see the little girl dead, and didn't want to waste time singing hymns over her parents.

"Perhaps you should stay behind, Reverend," Wayne said. "You and Mr. Brennan can handle the disposition of the...um...bodies..."

"Oh, I don't think that would be good at all," Tom said. "We need every man we can get. You said it yourself, remember?"

"That's true, but our time is very limited..."

"We'll make time," Tom said. "We can help dig the graves together, you and me. It'll help you feel better about the men you've lost. You know, the one's you were so upset about a minute ago."

Wayne's face was just a shade lighter than a desert sunset. "Quite so," he said.

"All right, then," Tom said. "Lead on, Mr. Fenris, lead on."

The cool breeze was at their backs, so they didn't detect the smell of death until they were almost in Ned Taylor's yard. Once they were there, amid the ruined bodies and the buzzing of flies, the stench was overpowering. It was heavy and palpable. One could almost taste it.

Tom, knowing what to expect, had been braced for it. Wayne, however, seemed to lose some of his usual bluster. He grew pale and subdued. He focused all of his attention on the corpses of his lackeys, refusing even to look at the Taylors.

Joe Keefer was a different story. He collapsed into uncontrollable sobbing at the sight of Laura Taylor. Tom was torn between pity and disgust. He was tempted to be rough with the boy, slap him and tell him to grow up, to be a man. He was walking over to do just that when he allowed himself a glance at the corpse of the rancher's wife.

In life, she had been quite a beauty. Tom himself had felt a pang or two of jealousy when he saw her on Ned Taylor's arm. She was a friendly, outgoing woman, the kind any man would be proud to...proud to...

Tom suddenly became violently ill. He tried to get behind the barn, but he couldn't make it in time, and everyone saw him lose his breakfast. After it passed, he had trouble making himself move. He stood there for a moment, hunched over and shaking, hands on his knees. He felt tears coursing down his cheeks, and wondered if they were from the nausea, or the shame. He pulled a rag from his pocket, and frantically wiped at his face.

A heavy hand fell on his shoulder, and he looked up into the cool, dispassionate gaze of Wade Morgan. "Drink some water," the drifter said, offering a canteen.

Tom accepted the courtesy. "Much obliged," he said. "I guess maybe Mr. Fenris was right. Looks like it might be better without me in charge."

"Maybe so," Morgan said. "Guilt can affect a man's judgment."

"Guilt?"

"You know, for not being able to save these folks. I can see it's eating you up inside."

"I guess...that it's pretty obvious."

"Yeah, but you're gonna have to put that behind you. It's not like you could have done anything to prevent it, right?"

"Yes, that's right."

Morgan nodded. "Mr. Brennan brought a couple of shovels, and there's more in the barn. Are you gonna be able to help with the digging?"

"Yes, yes, of course."

Morgan turned to go, but Tom stopped him. "Wait," he said.

"Yeah?"

"Tell the others...Tell them we're not gonna bury Wayne's men next to the Taylors. We'll take 'em over there, next to the tree line."

"Seems like a lot of trouble. Your boss might not like it."

"I don't give a damn! Just tell 'em! If they don't like it, they can take it up with me!"

"I'll let them know what you said."

As it turned out, no one argued the point. Tom was a little disappointed. He was all knotted-up inside, and would have welcomed a fight. The work went surprisingly fast. Everyone put their backs into it, including Karlo and – to everyone's quiet surprise – his silent daughter. The only exceptions were Wayne Fenris and the Baron Von Engel, who never stepped down from their horses.

When the bodies were covered, Hayes asked if he could say a few words. Tom knew that Wayne was fairly screaming inside at the delay, so he encouraged the Reverend to take his time.

"When something like this happens," Hayes said, "we are always troubled by the same questions. How could a loving God allow such a thing? How could He stand by while these innocent people were tortured and murdered?

"I wish I knew the answers, but I do not. However, I take solace in the sure and certain knowledge that right now – right this very moment – Ned and Laura Taylor are walking together in a place where pain and suffering do not exist. The horrors that they endured are just fading memories, soon to be crowded from their minds by the joys of Heaven.

"I also know that God has seen fit to draw us together to rectify what happened here; to bring the justice of this world to the killers who destroyed this family. Soon, those evil men will have to face their maker with the blood of the innocent dripping from their hands. What will they say to Him? What excuse will they offer?"

"No excuses," Joe Keefer whispered. Tom looked him, and was startled by the look of absolute hatred he saw in the deputy's swollen, red-rimmed eyes. Joe, Tom realized, was not the same person he had been a few hours before. It could happen that way sometimes, Tom thought. Something inside you breaks loose and everything just shifts around, falling into weird new configurations that grind and clank until the edges wear down. When it's over, when everything's settled in and knit back together, there's a new man standing there. Sometimes the new fella doesn't work as well as the old one, and sometimes he works a hell of a lot better.

Tom wondered what the new Joe was going to be like. He was certain that the kind-hearted kid he had liked so much – gangly and awkward and eager-to-please – was gone forever. He had been buried with Laura Taylor.

"I pray," Hayes continued, "those men will repent of their wickedness before that final judgment. While they breathe, they may yet atone. If they choose not to, they will find that whatever pleasure they took in their awful deeds was purchased with an eternity of hellfire."

"Amen," someone said. It sounded like Morgan.

The Reverend didn't say much more. He prayed for the safety of Emma Taylor, and asked God to deliver her safely into the hands of her rescuers. Then he called the three dead men heroes, and Tom thought he was going to throw up all over again. He glanced at Wayne, and saw that the man at least had the grace to look embarrassed.

When they were mounting up to leave, Tom noticed Karlo lingering by the graves of the Taylors. He held his hat in his hands, and his lips were moving in a silent prayer. Tom rode his horse toward him and coughed. Karlo slowly turned and looked up at him.

"Funeral's over," Tom said. "Let's clear out of here."

Karlo nodded. "Your assistant, Mr. Keefer, he tells me you were here."

"What of it?"

Karlo put on his hat. "The killers," he said, "how many were there?"

"Like I said, about ten or so."

"Were they all mounted?"

"What?"

"Were they all on horseback?"

"Of course they were! What kind of a question is that?"

Karlo looked around, then back at Tom. "A foolish question," he said. "I apologize for troubling you."

Tom didn't think he sounded very apologetic. "Why don't you go ahead and say what you're thinking, Mr. Karlo. I think I'd like to hear it."

Karlo smiled. "Pay no heed to me," he said. "I am an old man, prone to wild fancies." He walked past Tom and headed to his horse. Tom almost reached down and caught his arm, but checked the impulse at the last moment. Why push it? If the man was prepared to let it go, that was okay by Tom.

But what if he didn't let it go?

What was it he had seen?

Tom watched Karlo mount his horse. The man turned to his daughter

"Funeral's over. Let's clear out."

and made some gestures with his hands. She responded in kind, and they fell in behind the others.

"She's deaf and dumb," said Little Frank. Tom flinched in surprise. He had been so focused on Karlo that he hadn't noticed his approach.

"How do you know?" Tom asked.

"I been watching her."

"Have you, now?"

"Oh, yeah," Frank said. He smiled. "Have you got a problem with that?"

"I got a ton of problems right now, and so do you. I hope you're not thinking about making any new ones."

Frank's smile disappeared. "Don't you worry about what I think or what I do," he said. "That's my business, and you got no say in it."

Tom's eyes widened. "Just who do you think you're talking to?"

"A killer," Frank said, "just like me."

They stared at one another for a moment. Frank, satisfied that he wasn't going to get an argument, rode off and left Tom alone by the side of the graves.

Anton Karlo made a sign to this daughter that she should stay close to the Baron, then slowly worked his way to the front of the procession. He fell into step beside the man called Wade Morgan, and spoke to him in tones low enough not to be overheard. "Are you an experienced hunter?" he asked.

"I guess you could say that," Morgan replied.

"You are proceeding with great confidence, but I do not see you taking note of any sign."

"I don't need to, not yet anyway. The Sheriff already told me the last place they saw Sheldon's men. We're going there first. After that, I'll have to work a little harder."

"The Sheriff," Karlo said, "do you know him well."

"I just met him last night."

"I am wondering if he is being completely honest about what he saw yesterday."

Morgan turned his head slightly, narrowed his eyes. Karlo wondered for a moment if he had gone too far. He waited for a rebuke of some kind, but none was forthcoming. There was only a moment of contemplative silence. Emboldened, Karlo spoke again: "Does this not surprise you, what I am saying?"

"Not really," Morgan said. "I've been thinking the same thing, actually."

"You have?" Karlo said. He felt both surprised and relieved.

"Sure," Morgan said. "What tipped you off, if you don't mind my asking?"

"If his story were true, that would mean there were at least twenty horses present on the killing ground. I examined that area, and that is simply not possible."

Morgan smiled. "You remind me of a friend of mine," he said.

"This friend, can he read people as well as the ground?" Karlo asked. "If so, then I wish he were here. If I am correct, then we are surrounded by liars, perhaps worse."

"I don't think we have anything to worry about, at least for now."

"How can you be so sure?"

"Just a feeling," Morgan said. "Tell me, how many riders do you think actually passed this way last night?"

"Seven, possibly eight."

"Yes, Sheriff Henry and his friends. Soon we'll come to the place the Fenris boy was shot. What do you think we'll find there?"

"If my reasoning is sound, we will pick up the trail of one, two riders at the most. If they are not the killers, they certainly know who the killers are."

"My thoughts exactly. Until we catch up to those people, I don't think we have anything to fear from our companions."

Karlo nodded. "And when we do catch up with them?"

"I suggest you follow my lead."

"I will consider your suggestion," Karlo said. "May I offer you one of my own?"

"By all means."

"Do not play games with me. I am going to trust you for now, but you should remember that my daughter is a member of this hunting party. I will not allow any harm to befall her. Do you understand?"

For the first time in their conversation, Morgan turned so that Karlo could look him full in the face. "I understand," he said, "and I assure you that your daughter's safety is very much on my mind. In fact, nothing would make me happier than for you to take her right now and go back where you came from."

Karlo gave a rueful smile. "That would mean the end of the Baron Von Engel's patronage, I'm afraid."

"You could find another employer."

"It is not so simple."

"Why not? You're obviously a man with talents."

"And you are obviously a man with secrets. I am prepared to respect your privacy. I would appreciate it if you would return the courtesy."

"All right," Morgan said, and he turned away. Karlo continued to look at him for a moment. He thought the man might say more, but he didn't. After a few minutes, he quietly slipped back to his daughter and the Baron. Using sign, he told Valentine about his conversation with Morgan.

He frightens me, Valentine said.

Why? asked Karlo.

He is the only one here who isn't nervous. The others, they are all worried or excited or angry. Not him. He is like ice.

Karlo thought about it. *I see what you mean.*

He is a dangerous man, Papa.

So am I, daughter. So am I.

⁓❧ ☙⁓

"Funny," Gant said, "how it all looks different in daylight."

Tom Henry looked back at him. "What do you mean?"

"Well, this is the trail we came down, right?"

Tom said that it was.

Gant waved his hand around. "Don't it seem smaller now? Last night, I felt like the hills and the woods were closing behind us, like we were being swallowed up. Now it just seems like a scatter of rocks and trees. Not even big ones, at that."

Vance and Creed, who were just behind Gant, exchanged a look. "You sound like a little kid," Vance said. "It's all the same, dark or light."

"I dunno," said Gant. "Sometimes I wonder…"

"I do, too," said Creed. "I wonder if you're going loco. Next thing you know, you're going to be talking about ghosts and monsters."

"Don't you make fun of me, Charlie Creed," said Gant. "There was… something in the air last night. I didn't you hear you making any jokes then. You sure as hell didn't have anything to say when that masked man –"

"Shut up!" Tom hissed, but it was too late.

"What masked man?" asked the Reverend Hayes.

"One of the Sheldon Gang," Tom said. "The one who shot Jerry. He wore a black mask over his face."

"Was it Sheldon himself?" the Reverend asked. Tom noticed some of the others were starting to pay attention, especially Joe.

"I have no idea," Tom said.

"He was crazy," Gant said. "He said he was the Angel of Death."

"That reprobate!" the Reverend said. "An angel of Hell, more like!"

"What else did he say?" Joe asked.

"Nothing!" Tom said, with more vehemence than he intended. He cast a warning glance at Gant. "At least nothing that anyone could understand. It was a hell of a mess, guns going off, men yelling…"

"And Emma," Joe said. "She was there, too? You actually saw her?"

"Yes," Tom said. "This masked man, he's the one that took her. He's the main one. Maybe it *was* Sheldon, like the Reverend said."

"I didn't say that," said Hayes. "I was asking you."

"Yeah, well, maybe now you've got an answer," Tom said. He felt a trickle of sweat forming at his brow. Why the hell couldn't Gant keep his mouth shut?

"This man," Joe said, "was he dressed all in black? Did he carry his guns cross-draw, like Mr. Karlo?"

Tom saw the shock on the faces of Gant, Vance and Creed. He must have mirrored it, because he saw something flash in Joe's eyes that let him know he couldn't deny it or cover it with a lie. "He sure did, Joe. Do you know anything about this fella?"

Joe was opening his mouth to speak, but he was cut off by an exclamation from Morgan at the front of the procession. "What was that?" Tom said, grateful for the interruption.

"I said, is this the spot? Someone had a fire here."

Tom's eyes flicked around, and he realized they had come to the place where they encountered the Masked Rider. He rode up beside Morgan, who was already dismounting. "This is it, all right," Tom said.

The posse crowded into the clearing and watched Morgan wander around the remains of the fire. Occasionally, he would kneel down and press his hand to the earth, as if feeling for a heartbeat. After a few seconds of this he would get up, walk a few feet, then do it again. Tom had never seen anything quite like it. He looked at the other members of the posse, and they seemed as confused as he was.

"Well," said Wayne Fenris, "you see anything useful?"

"Dead body in those trees over there," Morgan said, inspecting the ground. "Other than that, not much."

"What did you just…?" Tom began, and then he saw it.

"Jesus," Gant said. "Is that Armando?"

Tom heard men dismounting behind him as he walked warily forward. There was a body there, all right. It was upright, lashed to a tree. A single arm extended from the inert form. As Tom got closer, he saw the wrist was tied to a low-hanging branch, creating the illusion that Armando – for it was indeed him – was pointing at something in the distance. The fear that had carried the man away was still present on his face, twisted and frozen in a never-ending silent scream.

"Why did he string him up like that?" Gant whispered.

Creed nudged Tom, then pointed to the ground at Armando's feet. Tom looked down, and saw that a message had been scrawled in the dirt:

THEY WENT THATAWAY

"What is that supposed to mean?" Creed said. "Is that some kind of a joke?"

By now the others had come to gawk. Tom turned and took in their faces. Their expressions ran from solemn to sickened to terrified. There was one notable exception.

"Hey, Morgan," Tom said, "You look a little bored over there. You're not interested in this? Is noodling around in the weeds telling you everything to need to know?"

"Just about," Morgan said. He brushed off his hands and stood up. He sauntered over to the gathering around the corpse, gazed impassively at the body, then looked in the direction indicated by Armando's dead hand.

"Hmm," Morgan said. "West."

"What about west?" said Wayne Fenris.

"That's where they're headed. That's where we need to go."

"Are you sure?"

"I'd bet my life on it."

"You may be doing just that," Wayne said.

There was an uncomfortable pause.

"What exactly do you mean by that, Mr. Fenris?" Morgan asked. "Am I to take it that you're going to kill me if it turns out I'm wrong?"

"I…I didn't mean…It was merely a figure of speech. Don't put words in my mouth, Morgan!"

"I just want to make sure I understand you," Morgan said, unruffled.

"Gentlemen, please," said Reverend Hayes. "We need to bury this poor soul. Here, you men help me cut him down."

"Excuse me," said George Brennan, "before we get started, there's a small matter concerning my fee…"

Everyone looked at him. "Fee?" Wayne said.

"Now see here," Brennan said defensively. "I was more than willing to allow you people the use of my excavating devices…"

"Your shovels," said Tom.

"My shovels," said Brennan, "which are the tools of my trade. Now, since no one else in this group has seen fit to similarly equip themselves, I see no reason – none whatsoever – that I should not be duly compensated for –"

"Oh, good heavens, George!" said the Reverend. "I can't believe that you would be so tactless!"

"No reason…" Brennan continued, undaunted.

"Fine!" Wayne said. "Fine! Fine! Start a tab! Whatever makes you happy! Now, can we please plant this poor bastard and get moving before the trail gets any colder?"

Tom and Gant severed the bindings and lowered Armando to the ground. Rigor had set in, so his arm could not lowered to his side without enormous difficulty. Somehow, the task of burying the dead tracker fell exclusively to Wayne's men. No one else seemed inclined to lend a hand, or maybe there just weren't enough shovels to go around.

What did you see, Papa? Valentine asked.

Only what I expected. The constable and his men had a confrontation here, but not with a gang of bandits.

Why are they lying?

I do not know.

Are you going to tell the Baron?

No.

At this, Valentine gave a slight smile. She despised the Baron, and grasped every opportunity to exclude him from the small, silent world she shared with her father. She looked across the clearing at Morgan, then back to Karlo. *The tracker, is he telling the truth? Is there a trail leading west?*

Yes, Karlo said. *Two trails, actually.*

What?

Both of them follow the same path. One is very fresh. Two riders.

And the other?

A few days older. Several riders.

The constable's men?

I do not think so.

Do you think the tracker can see the older trail?

I do not know.

Valentine looked at Morgan, and was startled to find him staring directly into her eyes. It occurred to her that he was somehow aware of their conversation, and the thought gave her a thrill of fear. Then her common sense reasserted itself. The language she shared with her father was their own creation, unique in all the world. He would have to be a supernatural being to understand it. On a whim, she raised her hands and made a sign to him: *Who are you?*

He looked at her quizzically, then raised his hands and made a sign in return: *Who are you?*

Valentine was charmed. The man was an excellent mimic. Not many people could have replicated the gestures after seeing them only once. Did he have any idea what he had actually said? Laughing to herself, she decided to continue the game. *No*, she said. *I asked first. Who are you?*

A dangerous man, Morgan replied.

Valentine gasped and turned to her father, but she saw immediately that he had missed their exchange. He was looking to the sky, lost in his own brooding thoughts. She looked back at Morgan. He tipped his hat, and offered a wry smile.

She felt her father tap on her shoulder. *Is something wrong?* he asked.

She pointed at Morgan. He was not looking at her now. He was rolling a cigarette, an activity which seemed to consume his full attention.

What about him? Karlo asked.

What, indeed? Had she really seen what she thought she had seen? It didn't seem possible…

Daughter?

It is nothing, Papa. Nothing at all.

Karlo shrugged and resumed his examination of the clouds.

"I'm worried about Gant," whispered Charlie Creed.

It had been several hours of hard riding since they left the clearing behind. They kept up a grueling pace, occasionally slowing to a walk so the horses could rest. Subdued and silent, they obediently followed Morgan, blindly trusting that the "trail" he was following was straight and true.

But what if it wasn't?

That corrosive doubt was creeping more and more toward the front of Tom's mind. Wayne's plan had seemed at least moderately acceptable the night before, but then Tom's thinking was muddled by fear and anger. Now, riding toward the mountains in the cool, clear light of day, it didn't seem like an acceptable plan at all. In fact, it seemed like the most amazingly half-assed scheme ever concocted.

"Tom, are you hearing me?" Creed asked.

"I hear you," Tom said. "I just don't care."

No one had ever heard of Mr. Wade Morgan until last night, and now they were betting everything – absolutely *everything* – on the chance that "better than most" meant he was the best damn tracker west of the Mississippi.

Then, assuming all that worked out, they had to gun down the little girl and the Masked Rider before any of the innocent members of the posse caught on that things weren't exactly going according to Hoyle. That was going to be one hell of trick.

"Maybe you ought to start caring," Creed said.

Then, if all *that* worked out, they were going to have to find a way to explain to Joe and the others how the great Sheldon Gang got magically reduced to one masked lunatic, and now that he was dead, well, the job was over and everybody could just go home. Too bad about the kid. Them's the breaks.

"Creed," Tom said, "I've got a lot on my mind right now. Can you just leave me alone?"

Hayes and Brennan might swallow it, Tom thought. Morgan would probably be content with a payoff from Wayne. The foreigners? Screw 'em. Karlo may have suspicions, but at the end of the day he was just a toady for the Baron. As for the big German, well, Tom knew the type. All that jackass cared about was blowing someone's head off, or taking one for a trophy. He'd be okay as long as he got the chance to scatter some brains.

But Joe...

Joe might be a problem.

Tom felt a hand grasp his elbow. "Dammit, Creed," he whispered. "What have I got to do? Write you a letter?"

Creed didn't back down. "This is serious, Tom. Look at him."

Tom followed Creed's eyes, and what he saw made him forget, if only for a second, his dread of what might be coming down the pike. He clearly had a more immediate problem.

Gant was separated from the others. He was riding about a hundred feet away from the general procession. He was slowly shaking his head from side-to-side and appeared to be talking to himself, or praying. Whatever it was, he was putting a lot of passion and energy into it.

"Do you know what he's saying?" Tom asked.

"He ain't talking loud enough for anybody to hear. I went over to him a little while ago, and he told me go away."

"Has anybody else tried to talk to him?"

"Not yet, but..."

"But what?"

"I can tell the Reverend's worried about him. If he eases over there to offer some counseling, and Gant decides he's in a confessing mood..."

Tom nodded. He rode over to Gant and pulled his horse into step with the other man's.

"Never hurt anybody in my life," he heard Gant mumble. "Just went along with what Jerry said. He's the boss. Whole thing was his idea, not mine. I never even got a turn with the woman..."

"Gant," Tom said gently.

Gant did not look at him. "Leave me alone, Tom," he said.

"I can't do that."

"Why the hell not?"

"Because my ass is on the line, that's why. I don't know what's got into you, but you'd better get your act together before somebody hears some of this stuff that's coming out of your mouth."

Gant was surprised. "What are you talking about?"

"You're over here spilling your guts to anybody who gets within earshot. That's what I'm talking about."

"I am? I was talking out loud?"

"You didn't know?"

"I had no idea," Gant said. He looked like he was going to start crying.

"Is there something I can do to help?" asked the Reverend Hayes. Tom almost jumped out of his saddle. "Oh, I'm sorry," Hayes said. "I didn't mean to startle—"

"Go back to the others," Tom snapped. "Go back right now, you hear?"

Hayes looked stricken, but he obeyed. Tom turned back to Gant and saw the man had indeed begun to quietly weep. Tom ground his teeth in frustration. It was bad enough watching Joe cry over Laura Taylor. Now he had to deal with this.

"I can still hear him screaming," Gant blubbered. "Jerry didn't say we were going to burn him. He just said we were going to have some fun with the woman. He said that she would probably even like it..."

"Gant," Tom said, "if you don't shut up, I'm going to kill you right here and right now."

"I went over to him…and he told me to go away."

That got his attention. "You wouldn't..."

"I would. I'd tell the others that you went crazy and tried to shoot me. It would take some fast talking, but I could pull it off. I'm getting to be pretty good at that sort of thing. I'm taking lessons from Wayne."

Gant took a deep breath and seemed to get himself under control. Tom was relieved.

"I'm sorry," Gant said after a moment.

"I don't need an apology. I need to know that you're going to keep your wits about you until this thing's over."

Gant nodded. "I know, Tom. It's just...I can't stop thinking about..."

"There's time enough for that later," Tom said. "Right now, we got business to take care of."

"I don't want to kill nobody else, Tom," Gant said.

Tom sighed. "All right," he said, "When we catch up with them, you can just hang back. Stay out of the way."

"Will you really let me do that?"

"Yeah, but you got to do something for me."

"Name it."

"Keep Joe out of it, too. Trip him up, knock him on the head, anything, I don't care. Just make sure when the hell breaks loose that he's not in the middle of it. Can you handle that?"

"I can handle it."

"Good, now let's go back to the others."

"Tom..."

"What?"

"Do you really think we're going to get away with it?"

"Yes," Tom lied. "I do."

They made camp by a small creek just before nightfall. The temperature dropped with the setting sun, so they all gathered close by a small cooking fire. They made a meal of beans and hardtack and some surprisingly good coffee, courtesy of the Baron. The conversation was muted and trivial, until Wayne Fenris decided to focus on some essentials. "Morgan," he said, "how long before we catch up to them."

"Soon," Morgan said. "Sooner than I expected, actually."

Wayne brightened at this. "Really? How's that?"

"They're moving slower than I thought. It's almost like they want us to catch up."

"Well, by God, we'll be glad to oblige them!" Wayne said. He looked around for approval of this rousing sentiment, but all he got was blank stares. Disappointed, he pursed his lips and went back to his coffee.

"How soon is soon, Morgan?" Tom asked.

"If they don't pick up the pace, two more days of hard riding ought to put us right on top of them."

Tom nodded. He heard Karlo translating for the Baron, and the big German grunted his approval. *Oh, yeah*, Tom thought. *Better than shooting elk any day.*

"Hey, Joe," Vance said. "There's something I want to ask you."

"What's on your mind?" Joe Keefer said.

"When we were talking about that masked man earlier today, you acted like you knew him, or that you had at least heard of him…"

"I saw him once, a long time ago."

"You met Dan Sheldon?" asked Reverend Hayes.

"I saw a man like the one these fellas described," Joe said. "I don't know who he was, but he wasn't Dan Sheldon."

"I think I'd like to hear about this, if you don't mind," said Wade Morgan.

Tom leaned forward. He wanted to hear it, too.

"All, right," Joe said. "It happened in Texas, when I was just a little boy…"

Sheriff Wilson had disappeared. At first, no one thought much of it. After all, grown men had their own business, even lawmen. If the sheriff wanted to drop out of sight for a couple of days, well, no harm done as long as he didn't make a habit of it.

Then the days stretched into a week, then two weeks. Folks began to get worried. The sheriff wasn't a young man anymore. What if something had happened to him? Inquiries were made. Search parties were organized.

It was decided that someone should be appointed as an interim lawman until Wilson was found, but no one wanted the job. Putting on the badge would have meant having to deal with the Dolan Brothers, and that was something that only Wilson could do. The Sheriff had been getting slow, and maybe a little hard-of-hearing, but he was still a tough old buzzard who never backed down from a fight. He was, in fact, the only man that the three Dolans were genuinely afraid of. Only a month earlier, the old man had beaten the hell out of Dub Dolan, the eldest, right in the middle of the street. The twins, Lonnie and Johnnie, had come to Dub's aid, and ended up getting their clocks cleaned as well.

Some found it interesting that the sheriff had vanished only a week or so after this particular incident, but they didn't comment on it much. The Dolans had been a lot more visible and a lot more rowdy since Wilson had been gone, and they were apt to take it personal if someone made…implications. They were sensitive boys.

About mid-way into the fourth week of Wilson's disappearance, a stranger rode into town. He was a very unusual man. He was dressed in black from head-to-toe, and a black mask obscured his face. He gave every appearance of being an outlaw, but there was nothing furtive about him. Rather, he carried himself as man with authority.

He rode down the middle of the main thoroughfare astride a muscular black stallion, stopping only when he came to the empty sheriff's office. Then he dismounted, tied his horse to the hitching rail, and walked into the center of the dusty street.

"I am here," he said in a deep, resonant voice, "to settle accounts with Lonnie, Johnnie, and Dubrow Dolan. Does anyone know where they are?"

There was a moment of eerie silence. Almost all the activity in the street had stopped, as everyone became mesmerized by the presence of the man in black.

"What do you want with them?" someone found the courage to ask.

"They murdered Sheriff Ben Wilson," said the dark man, "and today is the day they answer for it."

"Now that is just a bald-faced lie!" shouted Dub Dolan. He had emerged from the saloon with a wide, confident grin plastered on his pock-marked face. He was flanked by the twins. They stepped off the sidewalk and stood three abreast in the street. The bystanders observing the drama began to quickly and quietly slip inside various darkened doorways. The one exception, unnoticed by all, was a small boy who took shelter behind a rain barrel in the alley next to the saloon.

"Just who the hell do you think you are, making accusations like that?" Dub asked the stranger.

"I'm the Angel of Death," the masked man replied.

Dub's grin slipped a little. He glanced at his brothers. They were both looking to him, as they always did, for guidance. "Well, Mr. Angel," Dub said, "I think you got hold of some bad information. Where'd you get the idea that me and my brothers did anything to old Ben?"

"The little Kiowa girl who saw you stab him to death told me all about it."

"I told you I heard something in them bushes," Lonnie Dolan whispered. He said it just loud enough for the boy in the alley to hear. The boy saw Dub give his brother a cutting look, then turn back to the masked man.

"Did you bring this little girl with you?" Dub asked. "I'm sure everybody in town would love to hear her story. She can tell it in that courtroom over there. It'll be interesting to see how many people take her word over that of three white men."

"I believe her," said the dark man.

"Well, you ain't exactly a jury."

"You're right. I'm the executioner."

Lonnie and Johnnie turned to Dub, the question written plainly on their faces: Do we kill him now? Dub gave them the answer by going for his gun.

There was a clap of thunder, and the twins dropped dead in the street.

Dub stood frozen, his revolver only half out of its holster, his mouth gaping in stunned disbelief. In front of him, the masked man's smoking guns were now trained on his head. In fact, he was certain they were aimed directly at each of his eyes.

"Who are you?" Dub gasped.

"I already told you," said the dark man. "But most people call me the Masked Rider."

Dub swallowed, clenched his teeth, and drew his gun.

It turned out he was right about the eyes.

⚜

"What happened then?" Vance asked.

"He got on his horse and left," Joe said. "That's all."

"Well, Tom," said Reverend Hayes, "is this the same man?"

"I don't know," Tom said. "We can ask him when we catch him."

"Easier said than done," said George Brennan.

"Why don't you put a sock in it, gravedigger," snarled Wayne Fenris. "That man's as good as dead, along with the rest of his gang."

"He didn't have a gang when I saw him," Joe said. "And he didn't seem like much of a friend to outlaws."

"*If* it was him," Wayne said. "Don't take this the wrong way, Joe, but I think time may be playing tricks on your memory."

"What are you talking about?" Joe said.

"For one thing, there's that little gunfight you just described," Wayne said. "There's no way that could have happened the way you said it did."

"How do you figure that?"

"No one is that fast *and* that accurate," Wayne said. "I'm the best shot I know, and even I couldn't do that."

"Well, there you go," Tom said. "If a Fenris can't do it, then no one can."

"Are you mocking me, Sheriff?"

"Would I do a thing like that?"

"I know what I saw," Joe said, "just like you fellas that rode with Jerry last night. You couldn't have got any of your details wrong, could you? I mean, you were there, so you know what happened better than anybody, right?"

"That's right," Tom said softly. "What's your point, Joe?"

"Nothing. I'm just saying."

Joe stared at Tom. Reflections from the flames capered and danced in the young man's eyes.

"Well," Morgan said, "we've got a big day tomorrow. I reckon we all ought to turn in, don't you agree?"

They did.

Just as the sun began to blaze over the horizon, Tom awoke to the scent of flapjacks. He pushed himself up on his elbows and saw Karlo busy at the fire, flipping a hotcake on a skillet. "That smells pretty good," Tom said. There was a drowsy murmur of agreement from the others, blinking and yawning as they rose from their bedrolls.

"Thank you," Karlo said. "It is a skill I have mastered in the Baron's service."

"You do his laundry, too?" Little Frank asked, grinning. "Shine his shoes?"

"I do what is required of me," Karlo said.

This was an opening Frank was unable to resist. "Is that a fact? Do you give him baths?"

Karlo, ignoring him, continued to work at breakfast.

"Do you clean his teeth?" Frank continued. "Do you wipe his –"

Frank yelped as a flood of cold water washed over him from a pail held by Morgan. He leapt to his feet, spitting a streak of curses.

"Oops," Morgan said. "Sorry about that."

"Not as sorry as you're gonna be," Frank said.

"Shut up, Frank," Tom said. "Go walk around a little. You'll dry off faster."

"You stay out of this, Tom! This don't concern you!"

Tom rose to his feet and stepped over to Frank. "I said, go for a walk."

"What if I won't?"

"Then you're fired!" shouted Wayne Fenris. "And you can pack up and go home!"

Frank looked as if he had been doused with a fresh pail. His eyes nervously darted back and forth from Tom to…what? Tom glanced over his shoulder, and saw what was on Frank's mind.

"I'm sorry," Frank said quickly. "I was just funning. I didn't mean anything by it. You don't have to send me back. I'm sorry. I'll go walk around, like you said." He stumbled away toward the edge of the creek, pulling on his boots as he went.

"He changed his attitude in a hurry," mused Brennan.

"My men know not to cross me," Wayne said.

He doesn't care about that, Tom thought, turning to fully regard the object of Frank's furtive scrutiny. *He just doesn't want to lose his shot at this little thing.*

Karlo's daughter, oblivious to Tom's gaze, sat cross-legged before the fire, busily wiping at something with a piece of oilcloth. Curious, Tom stepped closer. What he saw surprised him.

She had completely field-stripped one of Karlo's revolvers, and was methodically cleaning it with care and enthusiasm. She was even smiling a little. Soon the others began to notice, and they also started watching the girl. After a brief moment, she completed her task. In a series of swift and practiced motions, she began to reassemble the gun. Her nimble fingers moved so quickly that they were difficult to follow, and in a matter of seconds she was finished, giving the cylinder a final, satisfied spin before setting the gun aside.

"Marvelous!" Reverend Hayes said, clapping. Valentine must have seen the movement from the corner of her eye, because she looked up and was clearly surprised to find herself the center of attention. She looked at her father, and he spoke to her with his hands. As she listened, her face flushed with embarrassment.

"Please tell her we're impressed by her skills," the Reverend said. "There are plenty of grown men who aren't half so clever."

"I can name several right off the top of my head," Tom said.

Karlo smiled and relayed these sentiments to his child, then translated her reply. "Valentine thanks you for your kind words. She says that she is only being a dutiful daughter." He gestured to a stack of hotcakes, steaming in the cool morning air. "And now," he said, "let us break our fast before the food grows cold."

It was a good meal, made even better by some molasses the Baron had brought along. The man did have some uses, Tom decided.

After a time, Frank unobtrusively skulked back. Without a word, Karlo handed him a plate of food. Frank took it without offering any thanks. He cast a venomous glance at Morgan, but kept his eyes away from the girl. Once, he noticed that Tom was watching him, and he stuck his chin out in a way that made Tom want to kick his face in.

When they were done, everyone quickly packed up and readied their horses. Tom had just finished cinching his saddle, when he saw the Baron wander over to some trees near the water's edge. The man turned and barked something at his manservant. Karlo, looking uncomfortable, said something back that elicited a flood of Teutonic invective. Karlo's face reddened as he endured this, then he slowly nodded.

"What's he so mad about?" Joe Keefer asked.

"He is angry because I have expressed a desire not to follow his wishes."

"You?" sneered Little Frank. "That can't be true. I thought you did whatever was required."

Karlo's eyes narrowed. "You are correct, boy," he said. "That is exactly what I do." He turned to Joe. "Mr. Keefer, the Baron has taken a great interest in the story you related to us last night."

"My story…"

"Yes, specifically the part concerning the gunfight you witnessed."

"What about it?"

Karlo pointed at the Baron. "He would like to know if he is approximately the same distance from us now that the three brothers were from the Masked Rider."

Joe thought about it. "No," he said. "He's a little too far away."

"I am going to walk toward him," Karlo said. "Let me know when I am at the correct spot."

Karlo walked about six yards before Joe stopped him. Karlo gave him his thanks, then said something to the Baron. The big German grunted and reached into a pocket, producing what looked like a piece of chalk. He then drew circles on three of the trees. He stepped back to regard his work, then smiled and added eyes and a mouth to each circle. Satisfied, he shouted something to Karlo.

Karlo looked over his shoulder. "I trust it is clear to all of you what I have been ordered to do?"

For a moment, everyone was perfectly quiet. The silence was broken by Wayne Fenris. "Five hundred says you can't do it."

By now, the Baron had walked back over. Karlo related Wayne's challenge. The Baron laughed, his ample frame shaking with delight.

"The Baron says to make it five thousand," Karlo said.

Wayne blanched. For a moment he wavered, then he spit in his hand and held it out to the German, who gave it a vigorous shake.

"All right, Mr. Karlo," Wayne said. "Let's see what you've got."

Karlo nodded once, then turned and drew his guns and fired. The roar of the guns made everyone jump a little. No one had expected him to move so quickly, with so little preamble. As far as Tom could see, he didn't even take time to aim.

Karlo twirled his revolvers and deposited them in his holsters. He turned to the posse, his face grim. "Four shots," he said. "Two from each gun." He gestured toward the trees. "You may inspect the targets."

Karlo and Valentine did not go with them. When they returned a few moments later, the Reverend was the first to offer congratulations. "An extraordinary performance," he said, shaking Karlo's hand. "The finest shooting I have ever seen! I must say, however, that shooting out the eyes of the one in the center was a rather grotesque touch."

"Merely the terms of the challenge," Karlo said.

Almost all of the others offered similar kudos. The exceptions were Little Frank, who walked past Karlo as he were air, and Wayne Fenris. "Tell your boss he'll have to wait for his money," the rancher grumbled. "I didn't think to bring that much with me."

"The Baron expected that to be the case," Karlo said.

Wayne gave a derisive snort and stalked away.

As he was mounting his horse, Tom heard Joe ask Karlo a question. "Why didn't you want to do it?"

"Why did I resist the Baron, you mean?"

"Yeah."

"I do not like to be treated like a trained animal, performing tricks for the amusement of others," Karlo said. There was no anger in his tone. It was merely a statement of fact.

"One thing's for sure," Tom interjected, "you've proven that you're more than a match for the Masked Rider."

"That remains to be seen," Karlo said. "After all, trees do not shoot back."

⁂

Karlo sensed that the others were looking at him with a newfound respect. He was not an immodest man, but the knowledge gave him a certain satisfaction. He was especially gratified to know that he had pleased Valentine. She was proud of her father, and often frustrated that others did not hold him in the esteem she felt that he deserved.

The thought made him smile. He cared little for the opinion of other people, but Valentine was his world. In the future, he would not argue with the Baron's requests. If it would make his daughter happy, he would give a demonstration every hour. *I will shoot mosquitoes out of the air*, he thought, and chuckled.

"What are you laughing about?" asked Joe Keefer. The boy had been riding close to him for a couple of hours now. He had been watching Karlo very closely, as if he were afraid to miss any spontaneous displays of martial skill.

"It is nothing," Karlo said. "Merely a random thought."

"What you did this morning," Keefer said, "that was really impressive."

"Thank you."

"They teach you to shoot like that in Germany?"

"Not Germany. I am from Romania. I learned from my father."

"Romania? I don't know anything about that place. I never had much school."

"It is a beautiful country. I miss it a great deal."

"As pretty as this?" Joe asked. He made an expansive gesture, taking in the majesty of the mountains rising before them.

Karlo smiled. "Yes, it is as pretty as this."

"Why did you leave?"

The smile grew cold. "That is my concern."

"Sorry," Joe said. "It's none of my business. I was just, you know, making conversation."

Karlo sighed. "You have not given offense," he said. "My reasons are…"

What exactly? Too personal to share with a stranger? Perhaps, Karlo thought. On the other hand, perhaps a stranger – a transient companion in a foreign land – was the ideal confidante. How would it feel, he wondered, to discuss it out loud with someone after all this time? He came to a decision.

"Some time ago," Karlo said, "the Baron and a group of his friends came to my country to hunt for bear. I was hired to be their guide. Then, as now, Valentine accompanied me on all of my hunts. Three days into the expedition, one of the Baron's acquaintances attempted to force himself on her."

Joe's expression darkened.

"Yes," Karlo said, "I see you can understand how I felt."

"You killed him," Joe said. It was not a question.

"I did. It made for an awkward situation. I was fully justified, of course, but I was afraid. Not for myself, but for my daughter. If things went badly for me in the courts, what would become of her? It was an outcome I refused to even contemplate."

"So what happened?"

"The Baron Von Engel happened. He was, to my surprise, not in the least upset by the loss of his friend. He took command of the situation on my behalf. He used his money and influence to extricate me from my difficulties, but his help came with a price."

"Price?"

Karlo nodded. "In return for the Baron's assistance, he required me to become his servant for…an indeterminate amount of time."

"I take it," Joe said, "that you ain't exactly happy with that arrangement."

"It was better than the alternative."

"How long ago was all this?"

"Five years."

Joe looked over at Valentine. "She couldn't have been more than twelve."

"Eleven, actually."

"These people," Joe said. "What the hell's wrong with these people?"

"Whom do you mean?"

"Everybody," Joe said, practically spitting out the word. "Listen, Mr. Karlo, it seems to me that you've probably paid the Baron back with interest. Why don't you just tell him you quit? What's he gonna do about it?"

"It is a debt of honor. I accepted the terms, and now I have to live by them, regardless of my personal feelings."

"Honor? You're crazy, you know that?"

Karlo was too surprised to be angered by this effrontery. "Why do you say that?"

"Where's the Baron's honor?" Joe said. "If he had any, he would have helped you without expecting anything in return. You don't owe him a damn thing, in my opinion."

"There is something in what you say, but I'm afraid it doesn't change my feelings on the matter."

Joe shook his head, exasperated. "That Baron," he said, "is no better than the man you killed. If you can't see that, then you're a blind man."

Karlo was beginning to get annoyed. "You should not be so quick to judge," he said. "You are still a very young man. You do not know what the future holds for you, what decisions you may be forced to make. When I married Valentine's mother, I thought I would be spending the rest of my life with her at my side, raising many strong and healthy sons. Three years later she was dead, and I was alone in the world with a little girl who could neither hear nor speak."

Joe was embarrassed. "I'm not trying to find fault with you," he said. "I didn't mean for it to come out like that. I'm just saying that you don't have to live like this if you don't want to, that's all."

"What I want became irrelevant a long time ago," Karlo said. "It is different for you. You have your youth and freedom, but time will pass and that will change. Soon enough, the responsibilities and obligations will settle on you like snowfall. You will see."

"You sound like Tom. He says stuff like that to me all the time. He's always telling me to live it up while I've got the chance..." Joe's voice dwindled into silence. He was staring ahead of him, his eyes boring into the back of Tom Henry's head.

"The Sheriff is a good friend of yours?" Karlo said.

"My friends don't lie to me," Joe said quietly.

"You think that he is a liar?"

"I didn't say that."

"I believe that you did."

Karlo half-expected the young man to round on him in a fury, but he only frowned. "There just aren't enough bodies," he whispered.

"I beg your pardon?"

"Day before yesterday, Tom and nine other fellas ride out to the Taylor place. When they get there, they have a shootout with ten or twelve outlaws." Joe looked at Karlo. "That's twenty or more men all blasting away. Must have been one hell of a gunfight."

"Indeed," Karlo said.

"Tom's group loses three guys, and manages to get Laura Taylor killed, besides. All of this without so much as wounding one of the outlaws. Then they follow this gang apace and get into *another* gunfight. Except this time, the bad guys aren't such good shots. They only get Jerry in the knee before they cut and run."

"That is what I have been told."

"It's bullshit," Joe said. "Tom can't shoot as good as you, but he still should have bagged some of those guys. And even if he went cross-eyed all of a sudden then *somebody* should have been able to put down at least *one* of the bastards."

"My friends don't lie to me," Joe said quietly.

"Unless, of course, they were not there to be put down," said Karlo.

Joe slowly nodded. "So who was? Jerry and the others sure as hell didn't shoot themselves. Don't even get me started on what got done to Armando. I still can't get my mind around that. Speaking of which, where's Mac? Everyone seems to have forgotten all about him. Is he one of the riders we're following? And what about the Masked Rider? Where does he fit in to all this?"

For a moment, they rode in silence. Then Karlo said, "I, too, have had questions about the Sheriff's story. But I had not thought of the things you mention. You are, I think, a very clever young man. Very perceptive."

Joe looked at him, blinking in surprise. "You mean that?"

"Of course."

For a moment, the anger and suspicion that creased the Deputy's features faded away, and Karlo could see the carefree boy he must have once been. "I appreciate that," Joe said. "I been called lots of things, but not smart. Never that."

Karlo smiled. "Well, I suppose now you have. Tell me, what is your opinion of Mr. Morgan?"

Joe's brow furrowed. He looked ahead to the front of the procession where Morgan rode, leading them into the looming mountains. "I don't know," he said. "At first he seemed okay, but now I'm not so sure. I think the only people I can trust out here are the ones I recruited myself. Maybe not even them." He gave a sidelong glance at Karlo. "Nothing personal."

"It is all right. I understand."

"Right now, all I really care about is getting Emma back, y' know? That's the only thing that really matters. But I'm gonna tell you something. After she's safe, I'm gonna get some answers. Somebody's going to tell me what really happened at that ranch."

The young man's eyes settled once again on the Sheriff.

"And then," Joe said, "some people are going to die."

At sunset they came to a ravine, a rocky incline about twelve feet deep bottomed by a narrow stream. There was some discussion, and it was decided that it would be better to traverse it in the morning when the animals were fresh.

Karlo took a few moments to walk along the edge of the ravine. He knew their quarry had passed here, but at what place did they cross? He felt very tired, and his mind wandered as he gazed at the steady flow of the cold, clear water below.

"This is where they went down," Morgan said.

Karlo looked to his right and saw the man, sitting on a small boulder, rolling yet another of his endless cigarettes. He walked to where Morgan was resting, and looked down the edge of the incline. He saw that Morgan was right. The sign was, to a trained eye, clear and very fresh.

"I think," Karlo said softly, "this hunt will end tomorrow."

Morgan, without turning his head, nodded.

"The expedition is being led by an excellent tracker," Karlo said.

"Thank you," said Morgan.

"I was not referring to you," said Karlo.

Morgan looked at Karlo, and smiled. "What do you mean?"

Karlo did not return the smile, but he kept his voice neutral. "I am speaking of the person – persons, actually, for I believe there are two – we have been following since we left the clearing, the one with the helpful corpse pointing west. These are the people who have *really* been tracking the outlaws. They are riding just ahead of us, intentionally leaving a very clear trail. A trail which you have been following."

Morgan said nothing.

"I observe this phenomenon," Karlo said, "and I ask myself, are these people in league with the Sheldon Gang? I doubt it. Are they confederates of Morgan's? I believe they are."

"Hmm," said Morgan. He turned his head slightly, and blew a perfect smoke ring. It remained intact even as it lazily drifted by Karlo's head.

"Then I ask myself, what is Morgan doing? Everything he says to me is technically true, yet he tells me nothing. Are we being led into a trap?"

"*You* aren't," said Morgan.

Karlo noted the emphasis. "I think that is true," he said, "and that is the only reason you are still at the head of this hunt."

"Ah," said Morgan.

"Still, I am presented with a quandary. What should I do with this knowledge? I consider it carefully, and then I have a most edifying talk with the young deputy."

"He is a good man," said Morgan.

"Yes," agreed Karlo. "In the course of our conversation, he reveals that he, too, is plagued by questions and doubts, but then he says something which clarifies things for me considerably. He says that finding the missing girl is the only thing that matters."

Morgan nodded.

"This child," Karlo said, "is only a few years younger than my own daughter. I would see her safe, if possible. If not, then I would see her avenged."

"Then we want the same thing," said Morgan.

"Perhaps," said Karlo. He glanced over his shoulder at the others. Valentine was rubbing down her horse. When she was finished, she would take care of her father's. It would fall to him to take care of the Baron's. "Morgan," he said, "I have trusted you for reasons which even I do not fully understand." He turned so that Morgan could see his eyes. "But if I discover that you have played me for a fool, I promise that I will kill you."

"Fair enough," said Morgan.

Little Frank couldn't sleep. He didn't carry a watch, so he had no idea what time it was, but he figured it was probably two in the morning. He laid on his bedroll, fingers laced behind his head, and stared up at the stars.

Tomorrow, things were going to come to a head. They were going to put paid to the masked man and the Taylor bitch, and if anybody in the posse had a problem with it, then they were going to eat a bullet, too. Old Fenris hadn't said as much, but he didn't really have to. Jerry's dad was one of those guys who wanted other people to take care of his dirty work, then sputter and fume about how that wasn't *really* what he wanted, that he never *actually* said to do anything like that. Whatever. If the arrogant ass made too much racket about it, then he could accidentally-on-purpose get shot along with the others.

Frank's eyes widened a little. Come to think of it, that was an interesting idea. Jerry sure wouldn't miss his father. He was always saying what a stupid blowhard the old man was. Would he really be sorry to see him go? Even a little?

Or would he be grateful?

Frank pushed himself up on his elbows and looked at the sleeping bodies that surrounded him. The fingers of his left hand lightly brushed against the scabbard of his hunting knife.

And why stop with Fenris?

He imagined himself rising to his feet and stealthily creeping to those bodies, passing over them like a shadow, and leaving each of them with a crimson half-moon carved into their throats.

He wasn't seriously considering this, of course. It would be stupid to take such a risk, especially with the Masked Rider still to be dealt with. Still, it was a compelling fantasy. The idea that he could do it, that he had the *will* to do it, was exhilarating. He realized with a start that he was becoming excited in…that way.

His eyes fell on the sleeping form of the Karlo girl. *I won't kill you*, he thought. *The others, maybe, but not you. I'm gonna keep you for a pet.*

The girl sat up.

Frank did not move. He did not breathe. He watched as the girl rubbed her eyes for a moment, then stood up and began to slowly tiptoe toward the trees.

What the hell?

Then he smiled as he realized what was happening. Little Miss Karlo was answering a call of nature. He quietly got to his feet, drew his knife, and went after her.

This, he knew, was the moment he had waited for, yearned for with such blazing urgency since the moment he had first laid eyes on her. Granted, he would have preferred a little more light and a soft bed, but he wasn't a perfectionist. He would take what he could get.

Still, he felt troubled by a nagging doubt. From some dim recess in his mind, he could hear the far-off echo of a voice shouting for him to slow down, to think for a second. This isn't the time, said this carping voice. There's too many people around. It's too dangerous.

How's it dangerous? Frank responded. *It's not like she's gonna call for help.*

But what about afterward? What if she tells her father?

She won't. The other one didn't.

But she might be different.

Frank shook his head, as if he could somehow rattle the voice out of his skull. He crept into the trees, and was rewarded by the sight of the girl close to the ground, her pants around her ankles.

Every muscle in his body felt taut as a bowstring. His heart hammered in his chest with such ferocity that it drowned out the night music of insects and wind-whispers. The only thing he could hear now was the steady drumbeat of his pulse.

This is a mistake, the voice whined. It was weaker, but still there, still insistent.

Frank gnashed his teeth. He recognized the voice, now. It was his own. The pathetic, lingering ghost of his old self; cautious, frightened, bullied into submission by life itself. In a word, *little*.

He stepped closer to the girl. He would catch her before she could stand up, knock her flat on her face, then show her the knife. She would under stand.

The voice made one last, feeble effort, muttering something about danger and being caught, but Frank barely heard it. That simply wasn't him anymore. His friend Jerry had opened his eyes to a world of pleasure and possibility that had had changed him forever, made him stronger, better, bigger.

She was reaching for her pants now, pulling them up.

Breathing like a steam engine, Frank advanced and was brought up short by a hand that wrapped itself around his neck and snatched him off of his feet, sending him crashing to the ground. A boot came down on his midsection, flattening his belly against his back and driving the wind from his lungs. The boot came down again, smashing his wrist and kicking away his knife. Now the boot was on his neck, pressing down, locking out the precious air.

Frank surrendered to panic. Every second that he couldn't breathe felt like a burning eternity. He tried to push the boot away, but his arms didn't seem to be fully attached to his body. His hands pushed and clawed with all the effectiveness of a bundle of feathers.

Goggle-eyed, writhing on a death-bed of dirt and pine-needles, Frank stared up at the night-terror that was taking his life. It was nothing but a shade, a patch of darkness shaped like a man in a Stetson hat, but Frank had no trouble recognizing him.

"Not this time, Franklin," whispered the Masked Rider. "Not tonight. Not ever again."

The stars seemed closer now. They danced and twinkled in front of his eyes like cinders from a guttering flame. He heard a light crunch of footfalls in the undergrowth, and he dimly realized it was the Karlo girl returning to bed, oblivious to what was happening just a few feet away.

The cinders began to fade as Frank descended into the abyss. He heard the distant scream of his little voice, the one whose warnings he had failed to heed.

Should have listened, he thought.

The voice, now gone mad with fear, offered nothing in return but a hysterical wail that dwindled into a whimper, and then silence.

Wayne Fenris looked down at Little Frank's body. The corpse was face-down in the water, head bobbing in the current. It had been spotted by Reverend Hayes just after daybreak. "How did this happen?" Wayne asked Tom, who had staggered down the incline with him to investigate. Tom reluctantly grabbed Frank and turned him over.

"Apparently," said Tom, "he got up to take a leak, and ended up slipping down the ravine. He hit his head on of these rocks, and drowned in the water."

"I guess that would explain why his fly's open," Wayne said.

Tom didn't say anything to that. He could think of other possibilities, but there was no point in voicing them.

"What a pain in the ass," Wayne said. "Now we're going to have to waste the morning burying this idiot. I guess that'll make George happy." Wayne looked up at the others, staring down from the top of the incline. "Hey, Brennan," he shouted, "here's another one you can add to your tab."

The undertaker, hat over his heart, responded with a solemn nod.

"You see that?" Wayne asked Tom. "That pompous beanpole really gets on my nerves."

"You're the one that thought it was a good idea to bring him," Tom said.

"Oh, shut up," Wayne snapped. "Here, hand me that rope and I'll tie it under his arms so we can drag him back up, unless you've got any better ideas."

"I don't."

"I swear, if I didn't have to keep up appearances I'd leave him for the vultures."

"It'll make Jerry happy that you buried him proper," Tom said. "They were pretty good buddies, y'know."

"To hell with that," Wayne said. "Personally, I'm glad he's gone. He was a bad influence on Jerome."

There was nothing to say to that, either.

Tom asked the reverend to keep it short, and he mercifully complied. Tom wasn't in the mood to hear a lot of sentimental platitudes about the dear departed. As far as he was concerned, Frank Pettigrew wasn't anything now but an unpleasant memory, best quickly forgotten.

Crossing the ravine was a dicey proposition, but they did it without any mishaps. Tom was somehow unsurprised to see that Morgan was emerging as the best horseman of the group. He and his gray roan navigated the hazards of the incline as if they were ambling across a parade ground. Tom commented on this, and the man merely nodded.

"Cutter's a good old fella," Morgan said, patting the horse. "My other horse, he's even better."

"Other horse?"

"Yeah, he'd walk into a volcano without batting an eye."

"Why aren't you riding him?"

"He had a more important job to do," Morgan said, and then he winked.

Tom forced a smile and fell back so that Morgan was ahead of him. He didn't like Morgan much, didn't care for his cryptic remarks and phlegmatic self-assurance. Still, he had promised that everything would end today, and if the next twenty-four hours proved the man right, he'd have earned every penny that Wayne promised him.

The terrain grew increasingly rugged, and the bite of the autumn air grew sharper. Although they were riding higher into the mountains, Tom had the disorienting feeling that they were somehow *descending*, walking deeper and deeper into a cold labyrinth of stone peaks and thick timber. He remembered Gant talking about how different everything was at night, and he wondered how this wild land would look and sound after the sun had disappeared.

Tom wasn't given to philosophical musings, but he felt himself being consumed by a melancholy sense of his own insignificance. He was forty years old now, and it was beginning to look as if the signature achievement of his life was going to be the slaughter of an innocent child. If Wayne's plan worked, Tom would escape a hangman's noose, but what kind of a life would he have?

Cut it out, he chided himself. *You can feel sorry for yourself later. Maybe you and Gant can split a bottle one night and have yourselves a little pity-party, convince yourselves you never had any choice in the matter.*

The thought made him look over at Gant. The man was slumped in his saddle, slack-jawed and morose. Tom had a sudden premonition. He knew – knew with complete certainty – that Gant was going to kill himself. He might not do it up here, not while he was still being driven by his own fear and the momentum of Wayne's determination to save Jerry's worthless hide. But if Gant made it home from these mountains, if he ever again slept in his own bed, he would be curling up with the corpses of the Taylor family. Their ghosts were going to scream in his ears every single night until he would finally drown them out with the blast of a gun.

The force of this vision was so powerful that Gant seemed to wither into a skeleton right before Tom's eyes. The skull turned to regard him with a hollow-eyed gaze, and Tom quickly looked away. Through sheer force of will he turned his mind to more mundane matters. He focused on Morgan, and followed in the tracker's steps as they led him onward and upward to damnation.

They spotted the smoke in the late afternoon; a thin gray tendril curling from behind a nearby ridge and rising into the sky. At first no one said anything, they simply regarded it as though it were some fugitive artifact from a collective dream, like a sign-post pointing the way to El Dorado.

"It's their campfire, isn't it?" Wayne asked Morgan. He was whispering, as if he was afraid of being overheard.

Morgan nodded. "I believe it is. They've gotten cocky, overconfident."

"Look there," Wayne said, "about a quarter mile northwest. There's a stream cutting through there. I'll bet that's where they passed through."

"I think that's a bet you would win," Morgan said.

"Hot damn!" Wayne said, a little louder now. "Hot damn, we've got 'em!"

"Don't count your chickens just yet," Morgan said. He pointed at the top of the ridge. "Why don't we ease up there and take the high ground. See what there is to see."

Wayne regarded the slope with a wary eye. It was not particularly steep or heavily wooded, but he shook his head as if it were a mountain of alpine proportions. "I don't think we'll be able to get the horses up there," he said. "Why don't we just keep on their heels, close on 'em hard and fast, go in guns blazing!"

Morgan rubbed his chin. "You know, Mr. Fenris," he said, "I think you've got a point there. May I make a suggestion?"

Wayne, pleased with Morgan's deference, was happy to oblige. "Go right ahead, Mr. Morgan."

Morgan looked at Karlo. "What kind of rifle is that the Baron's been carrying around?"

"A Martini-Henry with a telescopic sight," Karlo replied. "It is accurate up to eight hundred yards."

"That'll do," Morgan said. He turned to Wayne. "I think Karlo and the Baron should take the top of the ridge. We'll follow the stream into the valley on the other side. That'll put us riding straight into 'em. The Baron can hit 'em high and we can hit 'em low. What do you say to that?"

"Capital!" Wayne said.

"Hold on a moment," said the Reverend Hayes. "Don't you think we're being a little hasty? We're here to save a child, remember?" He pointed at Morgan. "Your plan might make for a good ambush, but it seems to me like a little more caution is in order if we want to bring that girl home alive."

Wayne, who did not want to bring her home alive, turned on the Reverend. "What exactly do you suggest?" he asked. "Go in under a flag of truce? Open up negotiations? You can't reason with these animals!"

"I didn't say anything about negotiating," Hayes protested. "I just think that –"

"You're not thinking at all!" Wayne said. "What you're doing is dithering, plain and simple. There's no time for that! This is the time for action, isn't that right, Morgan?"

"Yes," Morgan said. "It's time for action."

"But the danger…" said Hayes.

"Confound it!" Wayne said. "There's only one man…one or two men more than what we have here! And we have the advantage of surprise. Isn't that right, Morgan?"

"Yes," Morgan said. "The killers are in for one hell of a surprise."

"Damn right!" Wayne said. "We'll cut through them like a knife through butter and scoop that girl up before they even know what's happening!"

Vance, seeing an opportunity to suck up, leapt into the breach. "Mr. Fenris is right," he said. "Let's quit wasting time talking about it!" Gant and Creed, not to be outdone, chimed in with their own noises of approval.

"Mr. Fenris," Morgan said, " I think that maybe the Reverend and Mr. Brennan should sit this one out. This isn't work for them."

Wayne immediately saw the advantages of this. He'd had plenty of time to think it over on the trail, and he knew it would be best if there were no weak sisters in at the kill. There were enough men here to get the job done. "I agree completely," he said.

Brennan was secretly pleased to hear this. He had spent a lifetime making dead men presentable, and had no desire to risk becoming one himself. For the sake of his pride, he attempted to appear shocked and angry, but the expression was so lacking in conviction that he just looked like he was pouting.

Hayes, on the other hand, was genuinely wounded. "Now wait just a minute!" he said. "This is outrageous! I didn't come all this way to be pushed aside like some…like some…"

"Reverend," Morgan said softly, "how many men have you killed?"

Hayes physically recoiled from the question. "None," he said.

"Why don't we keep it that way?"

"But I want to help! I know that child! I knew her parents!"

"Then for their sake, let men with experience handle this."

Tom weighed in. "He's right, Reverend. This sort of thing just isn't your line. Best if you hang back." He looked at his deputy. "You too, Joe."

"No!" Joe shouted. "You're not shutting me out of this, Tom! You can forget that right now!"

"This isn't something I want you in the middle of, Joe. You're not ready for it. Now, I am giving you a direct order to stay with Brennan and the Reverend. Do you understand?"

"Go to Hell!"

Tom closed with Joe and drove his fist into the young man's jaw, knocking him from the back of his horse. Before Joe could get to his feet, Tom had dismounted and kicked him in the side of his head, sending him sprawling. He didn't move again.

The others observed this sudden violence with silent astonishment. Tom knelt beside Joe for a moment, then stood up. "He'll be all right," he said to no one in particular. He turned to Gant. "You're gonna stay with him, make sure he does as he's told. You got that?"

"I'll take care of him," Gant said, and Tom could see the gratitude in his eyes.

"I am wondering," said Karlo, "if that was entirely necessary."

"Keep wondering," Tom said. "I did it for his own damn good. Stupid kid."

Karlo looked as if he wanted to say more, but he was cut off by some querulous chatter from the Baron. Karlo responded with a staccato burst of German, and the Baron's flowing moustaches lifted with a grin.

"What's he so happy about?" Tom asked.

"I have explained to him what is happening. He is quite amused, and pleased that we are finally to have some bloodshed."

Tom looked at the Baron and shook his head, not bothering to hide his disgust. He knew he was being a hypocrite, but he didn't care. He wasn't out here for fun, and figured he could afford to look down his nose at someone who was.

Von Engel only laughed. He pointed at the ridge and said something to Karlo.

"The Baron wants to know if we are ready to get started," Karlo said.

"We'll all ride together 'til we get to the foot of the ridge," Wayne said. "That's where we'll split. Karlo, you and the Baron can leave your horses and head to the summit. I guess you'll want your kid with you, too."

"She does not leave my sight."

"Well, she ought to be safe enough up there. Anyway, it's not too steep. I don't think it'll take you very long to reach the top. We'll keep an eye on you. When you're ready for us to make our move, just wave a handkerchief. That'll be our signal. When we see it, we'll move along the base of the ridge to the stream, and then we'll follow it to their camp. I think you'll have a clear view of the action. When we start shooting, feel free to blast away."

Karlo frowned. "And if it turns out that these aren't the people we're looking for?"

Wayne held up his hands. "Then we'll walk up and introduce ourselves and ask them if they've seen any outlaws passing by."

Karlo turned to Morgan. "Do you endorse this plan?"

"It's the plan we've got," Morgan said.

"Remember my promise," Karlo said.

"Don't worry. I'll remember."

It was about an hour before sunset when Wayne saw Karlo wave his handkerchief. Smiling, he looked at the others. "Let's go," he said.

He started riding northwest with Tom, Vance, and Creed. Morgan, surrendering the lead to the rancher, was last in the procession. They left behind a scowling Hayes, along with a perfectly content Brennan and Gant, and the still unconscious Joe Keefer.

The stream was wide but shallow. It flowed like liquid crystal between the high walls of the ridge it had bisected, creating a long and shadowy avenue filled with echoes of rippling water.

Wayne turned to the others. "It's too rocky here to take the horses in at a run," he said. "I think it would be better if we just went in on foot. We'll sneak up on 'em, and open up like's Hell's own fury before they even know we're there."

Everyone quietly assented. They dismounted, and walked over the cold, hard stones into the mouth of the pass.

Tom stridently avoided looking back at Morgan. This was where everything was going to get sticky. They had to take down the Rider and the girl before the tracker could protest. Between himself, Wayne, and Jerry's two stooges, not to mention the Baron, he was confident that it could be done. Still, he wished some convenient pretext could have presented itself for leaving Morgan behind.

"Tom," Creed whispered. He was walking beside Tom in a completely unnecessary crouch, as if he were creeping behind a hedgerow.

"What?" Tom answered.

"Something's bothering me."

"Only just now?" Tom asked.

"Don't be such a smartass. Why have you always got to be that way?"

"Forget it. What's on your mind?"

"I keep thinking about what Karlo said. What if this isn't them?"

And there it was. The fear that had coiled like a dormant snake at the bottom of Tom's brain since the start of the expedition. What if Morgan didn't know what he was doing? What if he had been leading them on a snipe hunt?

"Well?" Creed said.

"Then I'm going to put one in Morgan's head," Tom said. "And we start over from scratch."

They were approaching a bend in the stream.

Just around those rocks, Tom thought. *Just around that corner.*

Now they were all crouching, slouching forward like monkeys with guns. Tom did it, too, even though he knew it was ridiculous. He just couldn't help himself. He was glad the Baron couldn't see them through his telescopic sight, or Karlo through the binoculars he had hung around his neck before ascending the ridge.

Wayne came to an abrupt halt behind a large boulder that seemed to mark the point where the valley opened up on their left. He stiffened, and then his head dipped forward as if it had suddenly become too heavy for his neck.

The snake in Tom's brain began to stir, hissing and shaking its tail in a warning rattle. Tom came up behind Wayne and looked over his shoulder into the wide, sunlit space beyond, the space that was occupied a scattering of trees, a few large rocks, and a group of about twelve armed men who were milling about the bank of the stream. Tom could smell the fish they were cooking over the fire. It smelled pretty good. Brook trout, probably. Fresh caught.

"Who the hell are these people?" Wayne hissed.

"The people you hired me to track down," Morgan said.

Tom turned to see that Morgan had his guns trained on them. He seemed a little taller now, somehow, and he was smiling.

"What is this?" Wayne said. He was keeping his voice low, but he was straining with the effort.

"The end of the trail," Morgan said. "Congratulations. You've found the Sheldon Gang."

Tom sighed. He felt as if he were deflating, like a leaky balloon. It was all so obvious. Why hadn't he seen it before?

It wasn't at all clear to Wayne. His eyes were too clouded with rage. "This is…I don't…What about the little girl? What about the Masked Rider?"

Morgan's eyes burned with the impossible glow of a flame encased in ice.

"We've found him, too," Tom said.

Understanding dawned on Wayne's features. "You bastard," he said, his voice little more than a gasp.

Vance and Creed, struck dumb with terror, had backed away from Morgan until they were almost touching Tom and Wayne. Creed was actually trembling.

Wayne kept his eyes on Morgan. "There's four of us and only one of you," he said. "Our guns are clear of their holsters. Your advantage is mighty slim, my friend."

"It's more than enough, Wayne Fenris."

Tom glanced at Wayne and watched the rancher's anger make war with his fear. It was a stalemate, leaving the man in a state of paralysis. Tom looked at Morgan and said, "So, what happens now?"

"You've got work to do," Morgan said, and he fired a shot over their heads. The echo of the blast seemed to go on and on, rebounding back on itself, redoubling, filling the entire world. At last it faded into silence, and was replaced by angry shouts, and a hail of gunfire that began to rain down on their position.

Tom and the others turned back to the valley, and saw men taking cover behind rocks and trees and horses, blasting away with rifles and handguns.

Behind him, he could hear Morgan speak. "It's just like you said, Thomas. There's nothing for you but to see it through to the end. If you try to run, I'll be waiting."

Tom looked back, but Morgan was gone. A bullet whistled past his ear and hit Vance between the eyes, blowing out the back of his head like an overripe tomato. Creed, his face spattered with little bits of Vance, looked at Wayne and screamed, "What now? What do we do now?"

Wayne set his jaw and started to return fire. "We shoot our way out of

"The end of the trail," Morgan said.

here!" he yelled. "Then we kill that son of a…" The last was lost in a thunder of guns.

"Endlich!" said the Baron Von Engel, and he pulled the trigger on the outlaw he had been aiming at since settling in at the top of the ridge. He barked a single laugh of exultation as he saw the man's head explode in the crosshairs of his scope.

Karlo, watching through his binoculars, muttered some words of congratulations. He had encouraged the Baron to target the leader of the outlaws, a man Karlo had recognized from a poster that Deputy Keefer had shown him earlier, but the Baron had ignored him, his strategic sense giving way before his natural contrariness.

One person that Karlo had not spotted was the kidnapped girl. This, of course, did not surprise him in the least.

The Baron fired, scoring another hit. He laughed a little longer this time.

Where are you child? Karlo wondered. *You're one of the riders who led us here, of that I am certain. But did you do so willingly? And if so, why?*

The Baron fired. *"Ha! Wunderbar!"* he exclaimed.

Karlo knew that Morgan held the answers. Every thread of the web led back to him. Karlo began to feel a cold fury toward the man. *I told you not to play games with me,* he thought. *The next time we talk, you will speak plainly. No more riddles and double-talk.*

The Baron fired. *"Ein weiterer treffer!"* he roared, and he happily punched Karlo in the shoulder. Karlo turned to offer a compliment, and blood sprayed into his eyes as the Baron's jaw was blown off.

"I think my jaw is broken," said Joe Keefer.

Reverend Hayes knelt beside him and helped him to sit up. "I'm sorry this happened, Joe," he said. "I really don't know what Tom was thinking."

"That's okay," Joe whispered, casting a baleful eye at Gant. "I bet I know someone who does."

Gant, still on his horse and keeping a respectful distance, quickly became uncomfortable under this scrutiny. "Why are you staring at me like that?" he asked.

"I'm wondering why you're here instead of with the others."

Brennan spoke up. "The Sheriff told him to stay behind and keep an eye on you."

"Is that so?" Joe said. He struggled to his feet and tentatively opened and closed his mouth a few times.

"You shouldn't take it personal," Gant said. "Tom only did it cause he wants you to be safe."

"That was real thoughtful of Tom," Joe said. "I think I'll go thank him for it right now." He started walking to his horse.

"Don't do that, Joe," Gant said.

Joe ignored him. He gave the horse a friendly pat, checked the saddle.

"Joe," Gant said, "back away from that horse."

The saddle was loose. Joe tightened the cinch.

"George! Reverend! One of you make him stop!"

The preacher and the undertaker looked at one another and did nothing.

"Damn it to hell," Gant growled. He dismounted and stalked over to Joe, fists clenched. As he was almost upon him, the high country silence was split by a fusillade of distant gunshots. Gant paused and looked up at the top of the ridge. Thus distracted, he didn't see Joe's right fist driving into his stomach.

Gant immediately dropped to his knees, struggling to keep from vomiting. He looked up in time to catch Joe's boot full in the face. There was a sickening crunch and a white flash of agony as his nose went flat, squirting a gout of blood down his chin. He rolled onto his back, cursing and clutching at his face.

"You'd better sit still, Gant," Joe said.

Gant lifted his head and found himself looking down the barrel of Joe's revolver. "What the hell's wrong with you, Joe!" he yelped. "I was just trying to look out for you!"

"Yeah, you're a real sweetheart," Joe said. He pulled back the hammer on his gun. "You and Tom only want what's best for me, I'm sure"

The darkness at the end of the gun seemed to grow larger, almost cavernous. Gant felt as if he could stand up and walk into it. "Are you going to shoot me?" he whined.

"That depends. What really happened at the Taylor ranch? And I don't want to hear that bullshit about Dan Sheldon. I want the truth. Now."

Gant shook his head. "But that is the truth! It was the Sheldon Gang! They were with that other fella, the Masked Rider! They killed –" He was cut off by a bullet that smashed into his right shoulder.

"Try again!" Joe said.

Gant told him everything. When he had finished, he looked up at the horrified faces around him. They stared at him like he was a foot-long scorpion found nestled in a bedroll.

"Good God," whispered the Reverend Hayes.

"It wasn't my fault!" said Gant.

"Shut up," said Joe, and he shot Gant through the heart.

Karlo splashed water into his face from a canteen and wiped at his eyes with a handkerchief. His ears were filled with the Baron Von Engel's gurgling howls of agony. When his eyes were clear, he looked up to see the Baron, the lower part of his face a crimson ruin, rising to his feet. The big German staggered to the ridgeline, his arms upraised as if begging for succor from the merciful God. A scarlet hole appeared in his chest and he collapsed in silence, his prayer answered.

Karlo rolled onto his stomach and saw Valentine where he had left her, safely behind a large tree about twenty feet down the eastern side of the slope. She was peeking at him from behind the trunk, her eyes speaking eloquently of her fear.

Stay there, he told her. *I am not injured.*

Let's get away from here, she implored. *The Baron is dead. There is no reason to stay.*

Karlo shook his head. He did not want his steps to be dogged by these outlaws. They had to be crushed here and now. He crawled over to the Baron's rifle and cautiously took up a position on the ridgeline. He scanned the fray below until his crosshairs passed over a figure hunched behind a boulder. The figure held a long-barreled rifle pointed in Karlo's general direction. There was a puff of smoke from the end of the barrel, and Karlo heard the bullet smack into a tree behind him. The figure lifted its head, and Karlo smiled in recognition. *The Baron should have listened to me*, he thought. *If he had shot the bandit-chief as I advised, he might be alive right now.*

Karlo squeezed the trigger, and entered the books as the man who killed Happy Dan Sheldon.

"Why don't we just make a run for it?" Creed yelled.

"Do you want to face Morgan with these guys at your back?" Tom asked.

"Less talking and more shooting!" Wayne bellowed. "Can't you idiots see that we're going to win this thing? The German's already killed at least five of them, and we've bagged two. By God, I think we can wipe them all out if they don't break and run!"

Tom, amazed, could only shake his head. Wayne's blood was running so hot that he had practically forgotten why they were here in the first place. It was enough to make you think they really *had* been hunting the Sheldon Gang.

"To hell with this!" Creed said. "He's just one guy! I'd rather go up against him than stay in this hornet's nest!"

"Dammit, Creed!" said Wayne. "If you run away from here, I swear I'll kill you myself!"

"No, you won't," Creed said, and he shot Wayne in the head. The rancher fell to a boneless heap at Tom's feet. He did not die immediately. Tom could see a faint, stubborn gleam that remained in the man's eyes. After a second the eyes fixed on Tom, and the bottomless despair he saw in them chilled him to the core.

"All right, Tom," Creed said, "how about you? Are you gonna try to make me stay?"

"Do whatever you want," Tom said. He was still looking at Wayne, watching the spirit that animated his massive frame fade and disappear.

Creed turned and started stumbling away over the wet rocks that lined the bank of the stream.

Tom turned his attention back to the outlaws in time to see another one go down under the withering fire of the German's rifle. Tom decided that he no longer had a problem with the Baron. In fact, he was beginning to practically adore the man.

Tom heard a shot behind him, and turned to see Creed falling into the stream, blood flowing from a hole in his chest. Standing over the body was the silhouette of a tall, dark figure; a walking shadow in a Stetson hat.

I guess there's no backing out until the job's finished, Tom thought. he chanced a look into the clearing, and saw that the job was closer to being finished than he had dared to imagine. Of the outlaw band, there were only five men still moving. Tom could hear the tension in their voices as they shouted at one another. He realized they were having a very similar argument to the one which had just taken place between Wayne and Creed. Tom allowed himself a giddy hope that it would end the same way. God, wouldn't that be sweet! If only the bastards would just shoot each other and get it over with!

Then one of them went flying in a mist of blood just as the sound of the Baron's rifle came echoing through the valley. That settled the argument for the other four, and they leapt to their horses.

"That's right," Tom whispered. "Run for it!"

As if obeying his command, they turned their horses and Tom grinned as he watched their backs begin to head away. Then came a series of shots from the other side of the valley. One of the outlaws was blown from his horse, and the others made an about face and started running straight at Tom.

"Oh, hell," Tom groaned. He crouched as low as he could behind the boulder as they went thundering by. It was a poor decision on the part of the outlaws. Wayne had been right about the rocky terrain in the pass carved by the stream, and it would be a miracle if the horses could make it into the plain beyond without coming up lame.

Suddenly, something made the outlaws pull their mounts up short. The horses whinnied and cried as they slipped and staggered, trying to find purchase on the stones.

"Who the hell are you?" one of the outlaws yelled.

Tom couldn't hear the reply, but he didn't need to.

A moment later came four shots that sounded as one, and the last of the Sheldon Gang was keeping Creed company, their blood mixing and mingling with his, trickling in red rivulets into the stream.

Who the devil fired those shots? Karlo wondered. He turned his scope to the western end of the valley, his finger tense on the trigger. A moment later, he found what he was looking for.

A red man armed with a lever-action rifle came into the crosshairs. He was lithe and muscular, with raven black hair tied in twin braids. He was mounted on a beautiful sorrel mare, and he rode with the dignity of a Roman general at the head of a triumph. Karlo followed him with the rifle for a moment, and then the man paused. He slowly turned and looked directly at Karlo. His face was stern and middle-aged, and his black eyes flashed in the glow of the evening sun.

Can you see me? Karlo thought.

The man raised his left hand, and slowly waved.

I suppose you can.

Then someone else rode into his field of vision. It was a little girl, not many years younger than his own daughter. She was mounted on a muscular black horse, as magnificent an animal as Karlo had ever seen. She exchanged a few words with the red man, who pointed at the top of the ridge. She followed his finger, and looked into Karlo's eye.

Karlo smiled. *Hello, Miss Taylor.*

He stood up, gestured for Valentine to follow, and began to descend the ridge into the valley.

Tom was shaking. The adrenaline was racing through his body like lightning, making his muscles dance beneath his skin. He was, incredibly, still alive, and not even so much as scratched.

But for how long?

The man in black was approaching. His gait was steady, unhurried, implacable. The red evening light that illuminated the pass seemed unable to touch him, as if he was made up of a darkness so deep that the sun could not reach it.

Tom holstered his gun and forced himself to his feet. He stood up straight, hands held open, and addressed the dark man. "You said we were all dead men. Looks like you were right."

The man in black stopped walking. He was standing about twenty feet away. He appeared now as Tom had first seen him. All vestiges of Morgan were gone, save for the pitiless blue eyes that stared out through the mask.

"Not all," said the Masked Rider. "Not yet."

Tom slowly placed his hands on his buckle. "What if I just dropped this gun-belt?" he asked. "Would you take me in?"

"Is that really what you want?" said the Rider.

They silently regarded one another. Tom's right hand slipped away from his buckle. Then he saw something over the Rider's shoulder, and his heart filled with a sunburst of hope. "Joe!" he shouted. "Shoot him, Joe! Now!"

Nothing happened. The hope dimmed, turned gray, and disappeared.

"Stand aside, Mister," Joe Keefer said to the Rider, and the dark man obeyed.

"Joe?" Tom said.

The echo of the shot was still ringing in his ears when he hit the ground. At first he didn't feel anything but the stones beneath his back.

What happened? Did I slip on something?

He felt a burning in his chest. He looked down and saw a smoking hole in the center of his badge. The burning began to grow worse, and was joined by a strange, internal pressure that seemed to be forcing the air from his lungs, pressing his heart painfully against his ribs.

He stared up at the sky, and suddenly a face was looming over him. It was the face of a child, a little girl with tears flowing from her eyes. One of them fell on his lips, and he could taste the salt on his tongue.

"Emma?" he whispered.

The girl did not speak. She stared down at him, quietly weeping.

"Help me," he gasped

"That's what my mama said," replied the girl. "Do you remember?"

Tom remembered, and then he died.

Anton Karlo walked through the dead men toward the strange gathering at the mouth of the pass. As he approached, he saw the red man watching him warily, rifle held loosely in one hand.

"Morgan!" Karlo said. "I would like to speak with you."

A masked man clad in black stepped away from the others to face him. "Morgan's gone," said the man. "But we can talk, if you like."

Karlo stopped. He was about the same distance from the dark man as he had been from the chalk targets the Baron had drawn in the trees. "I suppose you think you are a very clever fellow," he said. "Did you know that the Baron is dead because of your machinations?"

"That's too bad," said the Masked Rider.

"That's all you have to say?"

"He came out here to kill people for sport. He knew the risks."

Karlo nodded. "True enough," he said. "To be honest, I cannot say I am saddened by his passing. I am, however, somewhat irritated to know that I have been moved about like a chess piece. It is an offense to my pride."

"The first sin," said the Rider, "and the deadliest."

Karlo frowned. His hands were very close to his guns. "I warned you what I would do if you played me for a fool," he said.

Karlo narrowed his focus, and the rest of the world seemed to fall away, leaving only an island of tension occupied by himself and the man in black. Then he felt a soft hand close around his left wrist. He turned and looked into the confused and frightened eyes of Valentine.

She released his hand, and spoke to him in sign. *What are you doing?
I am having a discussion with this man.*

Valentine shook her head. *That is not a man who holds discussions.* She stepped in front of her father. *This hunt has ended. Please take me from this place of death.*

Karlo nodded, and pulled her to him. As she embraced him, he looked over her shoulder at the dark man. "It would have been interesting to know," he said, "which of us was the fastest."

"I hope you never have to find out," said the Masked Rider.

Emma Taylor was sitting on a small boulder by the side of the stream. A shadow fell over her, and she looked up into the blue eyes of her avenger. She smiled at him. "Thank you for letting me take your horse," she said. "He's wonderful. I don't reckon you'd let me keep him?"

"I'm afraid not," he said, but he said it kindly.

"I'll go with you to San Francisco, now. I mean, if you're still willing to take me."

"Are you sure?"

She nodded. "Joe and the Reverend said they'd look out for me, but I can never go to that town again. Never."

"I understand. You can go ahead with Blue Hawk. I'll catch up with you later."

"What are you going to do?"

"Nothing special. I just need to tie up a loose end."

Borne aloft on a morphine wind, Jerome Fenris soared over the wasteland of his imagination. His victims, past and future, wept and writhed beneath him, begging for his mercy. Jerome's mouth watered as he contemplated this feast of flesh, deciding which morsel he would pluck and devour first.

Then, through the cacophony of moans and cries, came unwelcome voices. They drifted over the red horizon, pulling him away from his pleasures and dragging him down to the waking world of fever and pain and sweat-soaked sheets.

I know what they did, someone said. Was that Purvis?

Then you know what has to be done, someone replied. The voice was strange, but somehow familiar. Where had he heard it before? It was someone he hated. A man in black.

Jerome remembered something, a threat he had made. *I'll see you again*, he had said.

You certainly will boy, replied the man in black, *and that will be the day I bear you off to Hell.*

Jerome opened his eyes, and saw a shadow at the foot of his bed. The shadow was holding a noose.

"Today's the day," said the Angel of Death.

THE END

Notes on "The Hunting Party"

Cinema buffs will have recognized that this story shares its title with a 1971 Euro-western starring Gene Hackman and Oliver Reed. The film's a bleak, nihilistic piece of work and I can't say I recommend it, but its basic premise—the pursuit of a sympathetic outlaw by a corrupt "posse" of depraved elites—made a lasting impression on me. My fascination with that idea has found its full expression in the present work. Although the plot of my story is completely different, I do pay homage to the movie by arming Baron Von Engel with the same Martini-Henry rifle used by Hackman and his decadent pals. Although I wanted to avoid winking at the reader in this story, I couldn't resist throwing in a few other salutes to the great Western movies I have enjoyed over the years. I've quoted a couple of great lines, and thrown in some character references that I hope made you smile. I'm afraid you score no points for guessing who Hayes and Brennan are named after, but I will send you a no-prize if you can identify the Rider's "friend at the Carlton Hotel."

Leaving behind the movies, there is also a literary influence that I feel compelled to acknowledge. It will be obvious to any fan of the classic pulps that my version of the Masked Rider owes an enormous debt to Walter B. Gibson's "Shadow" novels. Gibson's brilliant work remains the purest distillation of the "dark avenger" archetype. The idea of taking such a character and dropping him into a traditional horse opera is one that I found irresistible.

No writer works in a vacuum, and there were several people who played a pivotal role in the creation of this story. The advice and encouragement of my friend (and fellow Airship 27 contributor) Micah Harris has been invaluable over the years. Were it not for him, you would not be reading this now. Now you have someone to blame.

I also need to thank kung fu film scholar Ric Meyers. I met Mr. Meyers at a film festival during a time when I was suffering from one of the worst cases of writer's block I have ever experienced. I only had two brief conversations with him, but his passion and his energy (his *chi*?) proved to be very inspiring for me. I found myself thinking in different ways not only about this story, but my entire approach to writing. Soon, I was back at the keyboard and working harder than ever. I'd like to pay him back here with a sincere plug: If you have even a passing interest in martial arts movies, you should pick up Ric's book, *Films of Fury*. It really is a great read.

Finally, I want to express my sincere gratitude to Jean-Marc Lofficier. In 2006, Jean-Marc accepted a submission from me for his great *Tales of the Shadowmen* anthology series published by Black Coat Press (www.black-coatpress.com). It was my first time in print, and I can still remember the adrenaline rush I felt the day my copy arrived in the mail. I've worked for him many times since, and I have consistently found him to be patient, supportive, and unfailing in his critical acumen. This story is dedicated to him.

ROMAN LEARY - was eight years old when a family friend passed him an Ace paperback of *Conan* stories. He has been a devotee of pulp fiction ever since. His first novel, *Brother Bones: Six Days of the Dragon*, was published by Airship 27 in 2013. He lives in North Carolina with his wife and their beautiful daughter.

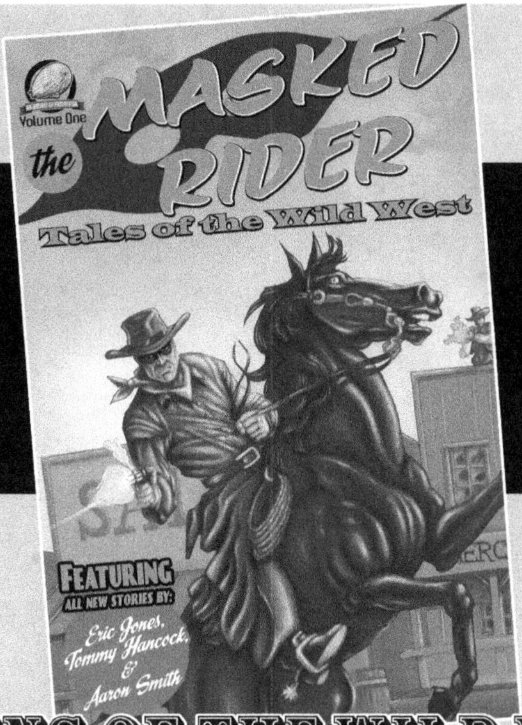

GUNS OF THE WILD WEST

Airship 27 Production saddles up to bring its readers three tales of gun-blazing justice from out of the old Wild West. In the years immediately following the Civil War, the land west of the great Mississippi River was a lawless frontier being shaped by the courageous men and women who ventured there in hopes of finding a better life. What they found was a vast wilderness exploited by outlaws, grifters and cattle barons who made their own law at the end of a gun. Caught in the middle were the brave and noble Native American people, struggling to survive against this tide of so-called civilization.

A rare breed of men took on the challenge of bringing justice the west; men like the mysterious Masked Rider, Virgil Earp and Wild Bill Hickok. These were men who cast their long shadows over western history and went on to become legends. Now writers Eric Jones, Tommy and Aaron Smith bring us their adventures in three fast paced, no-holds barred shoot'em ups wherein it's good versus evil on the dusty streets and rolling plains of this big country. Load your six shooters, pilgrims, and saddle up for western action Airship 27 style.

AN AIRSHIP 27 PRODUCTION

PULP FICTION FOR A NEW GENERATION!

AVAILABLE IN KINDLE & PDF FORMAT. LINKS AT: AIRSHIP27HANGAR.COM

AIRSHIP27HANGAR.COM

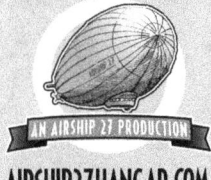

DEATHWALKER

TOUCHED BY DEATH

While on his vision quest, the young Cheyenne brave High Bird encounters the sprit of Death. The powerful wraith recruits the boy as his new agent in the world and High Bird returns to his tribe altered forever as Deathwalker. When the Cheyenne become the target of a vengeful Pawnee Shaman, Stands Alone, only Deathwalker can stand between this evil sorcerer and the total destruction of his people.

Writer R.A. Jones has woven a new and exciting fantasy set against a background authentic Native American lore and culture. He dares to imagine what this wild untamed land would have become had there been no conquests by outside civilizations beyond the great waters. Here is an old world re-envisioned in a bold new action packed adventure worthy of pulp writers such as Robert E. Howard and Edgar Rice Burroughs. Featuring stunning cover art by Laura Givens with interior illustrations by Michael Neno.

Airship27 is proud to present R.A. Jones' DEATHWALKER, another original and quality title in the New Pulp movement.

AN AIRSHIP 27 PRODUCTION

AIRSHIP 27 PRODUCTIONS – *Pulp Fiction For A New Generation!*
Available at Amazon.com and in PDF ebooks at Airship27Hangar.com